Puffin Plus

THE RETURN OF

'How can a team that's just been promoted be in deep financial trouble?' asked Boxer.

'For that very reason, son.' Mac's voice was very grim.

But money trouble was only one of the problems facing Murphy's Mob – Dunmore United F.C.'s Junior Supporters' Club. Wily chairman Rasputin Jones had bungled the all-important merger with Dunmore Town F.C., leaving the bulldozers flattening his club's ground, Mac Murphy without a team to manage – and the Mob without a clubhouse.

Still worse was to follow, as the Mob – determined to get to the bottom of this disaster – found themselves in trouble with the law, attacked by punks, and under threat of expulsion by their arch-enemy, smarmy, two-faced Cassidy.

Based on Brian Finch's hugely successful television series, this is another terrific read for fans of *Murphy's Mob*, packed full of humour, skulduggery, courage and adventure.

Murphy's Mob by Michael Saunders and *Murphy & Co.* by Anthony Masters are also published in Puffin Plus.

THE RETURN
OF MURPHY'S MOB

by Anthony Masters
adapted from the Central Television series
by Brian Finch

PUFFIN BOOKS

Puffin Books, Penguin Books Ltd, Harmondsworth, Middlesex, England
Viking Penguin Inc., 40 West 23rd Street, New York, New York 10010, U.S.A.
Penguin Books Australia Ltd, Ringwood, Victoria, Australia
Penguin Books Canada Ltd, 2801 John Street, Markham, Ontario, Canada L 3 R 1 B 4
Penguin Books (N.Z.) Ltd, 182–190 Wairau Road, Auckland 10, New Zealand

First published 1984

Made and printed in Great Britain by
Richard Clay (The Chaucer Press) Ltd,
Bungay, Suffolk
Filmset in Monophoto Plantin by
Northumberland Press Ltd, Gateshead,
Tyne and Wear

'Funny,' said Wurzel, 'I always wondered what it would be like.'

'What?' asked Jenny.

'The end of the world.'

The bulldozer lurched back and hit the wall again, sending bricks, dust and the final part of the sign – DUNMORE UNITED FOOTBALL CLUB LTD – crashing to the ground in a cloud of swirling dust.

'Come on,' sighed Jenny. 'This is a real downer.'

'Wait a minute. There's something I want to get.'

'We cleared the club of everythin',' snapped Jenny. 'What can you possibly want now?' She stared around the demolition site miserably. 'It's all goin' – or gone.'

'Not everythin', Jen – I'll see you in a bit, all right?'

'Wurzel –'

But he had hurried off into the white dust, not listening to her.

'Wurzel!' she shouted again, but he had disappeared from view. Shrugging, she decided to follow him.

When she caught up with him, Wurzel was trying to prise something off a door.

'What are you up to?'

Breathing heavily he wrenched – and wrenched again. Then the wood splintered and Wurzel fell back heavily on to a pile of rubble. Gasping, he lay there for a few seconds, his hands clasping a long strip of metal.

'Got it!' he said triumphantly.

'Got what?' asked Jenny irritably.

Wurzel held up his prize. It read: DUNMORE F.C. JUNIOR SUPPORTERS' CLUB.

Jenny's expression softened. 'Well – you are an old sentimental wotsit.'

'It's nostalgia, that's all,' said Wurzel, getting up and dusting himself down. 'Just a bit of nostalgia.'

Charlotte Masters, bent double under the weight of her rucksack, tottered down the aisle of the Inter-City Express towards the empty seat. Boxer looked up from his pop magazine as she reached it, registering both her prettiness and her exhaustion. She was about fifteen, with a determined look about her, and Boxer very much liked what he saw. So when she began to heave her heavy rucksack up to the rack, Boxer jumped eagerly to his feet.

'I'll do that for you.'

'No thanks – I can manage,' replied Charlotte in a superior voice.

'Right,' said Boxer in a tone that meant 'please yourself'. He sat down again and Charlotte continued to struggle with her bag. Finally, she settled down opposite him, only to catch sight of an annoying flickering grin on Boxer's face. Then he said calmly, smugly:

'That one's taken.'

'Who says?' she asked pertly.

'He does.'

'Who's he?'

'The geezer who filled out that ticket, I s'pose. You know, the one just above yer left ear.'

Looking up, Charlotte saw to her fury that there was a reserved ticket on the back of her seat – something she had not noticed in her confusion over the bag. Glaring at Boxer's bland stare, Charlotte tried to move into the window seat, only to find Boxer's feet in the way.

'Do you mind?'

'Sorry.'

Boxer reluctantly moved and Charlotte sat down suddenly, unsettled by the gathering speed of the train.

'Whoops,' said Boxer and Charlotte frowned, conscious of her loss of dignity. Boxer peered at her over the top of his magazine. She might be stuck-up, but she really wasn't bad looking. Charlotte glanced up fractionally to meet his gaze. She gave him a cold look, fiddled in her bag, brought out a can of coke with a plastic cup and began a shaky pouring routine. Boxer risked another glance at her as she sipped. Then he said:

'Fancy something to read?'

Charlotte stared down at his other pop magazines on the table.

'Help yourself,' said Boxer, a little too eagerly.

'No thanks,' she replied with sweet sharpness. 'I don't really fancy any of those.'

'Friendly little soul, aren't we?' Boxer returned to his reading, while Charlotte treated him to a disdainful stare. As he buried himself in his magazine, Boxer saw a headline above the photograph of a downhearted-looking boy of his own age. It read: DO YOU TURN GIRLS RIGHT OFF?

Derek Cassidy, manager of Outer Space Amusements – which was owned by Dunmore United's president, Rasputin Jones – watched his latest space-invader machine being played with great skill by a studious kid known as Pacman, ably assisted by a minute child known as Hulk. But the main focus of his attention was Wurzel, who leant against a wall, watching them play as if he had all the time in the world. Cassidy's eyes narrowed – he had been there too long, he wasn't spending any money and he didn't seem to be doing any work either. The telephone rang just as Cassidy was about to step threateningly out of his office, gaining Wurzel a temporary reprieve.

As he picked up the receiver and listened, Cassidy's smile became glacial. 'No – this isn't Captain Kirk. My name is Derek Cassidy and I'm general manager here. Can I help you? No – Mr Rasputin Jones is not here, I'm afraid. I've no idea where he is. The *Sentinel*? Yes – I'll tell him. Goodbye.'

Frowning, Cassidy returned to stare at Wurzel. Then, with a grunt of decision, he darted out of his office and into the arcade. He marched up to Wurzel.

'Expect that to collapse any moment, do you?'

'Eh?' Wurzel started.

'The wall – you're propping up the wall.'

'Oh,' said Wurzel, coming to. 'The wall – hey – that's good.'

'No, it isn't, Glossop. It would appear that you and I are at cross-purposes.'

'Why's that, Mr Cassidy?' asked Wurzel innocently.

Cassidy replied, slowly and menacingly, 'Yes. You see – I was under the impression that you were being paid to work here. Sweep the floor and do what you could in your own small way to keep the level of litter down. But as far as I can see, you don't agree with this.'

'No?'

'You see yourself in quite a different capacity.' Cassidy's voice was becoming faster and colder.

'Oh, yes?' Wurzel said uneasily.

'You see, Glossop, I think you visualize yourself as some kind of free-standing wall unit.'

'You're quite wrong there, Mr Cassidy.'

'Am I?'

'Yeah. You see, what's confusing you is my method of working.'

'Your what?'

'What you might call my modus operandi. Now, when you saw me leaning against this wall, I bet you thought I was skiving.'

'It would have been a safe bet.'

'But what I was really doin' was rechargin', see. For my next burst.'

'What next burst?'

'Of frenzied activity. You see, Mr Cassidy, with some people it's all on one level.'

'Is it?' asked Cassidy incredulously.

'But with others,' continued Wurzel slowly and calmly, 'it's peaks and troughs, see. An' I'm one of the others. One minute I'm loafin' about doing nothin' – the next I'm right in the middle of one of me bursts and doing the work of ten normal men.'

'Are you by any chance trying to take the mick, Glossop?'

'No, Mr Cassidy.'

'Then tell me something, Glossop.'

'Yes, Mr Cassidy?'

'You were taken on here by Mr Jones for reasons that I have to admit were best known to himself. It was certainly against my advice and I have to say that since starting work here, nothing you've done has given me any cause to change my opinion.'

'I'm sorry about that, Mr Cassidy.'

'So am I, Glossop. So I have one small piece of advice for you.'

'Yes, Mr Cassidy?'

'Watch it.'

'Right, Mr –'

'Or you're out. Out on your neck.' Cassidy picked up a broom and thrust it into Wurzel's hands. 'You have two minutes to get that rubbish cleared up. If – when I get back – I find as much as a toffee paper on this floor, your next frenzied burst will almost certainly be in the general direction of the nearest exit.'

Cassidy turned on his heel and stalked off. As he did so, the Hulk slid up to the grimacing Wurzel.

'Do you get the funny feeling he doesn't like you very much?'

'I get a funny feeling about him too –'

'What's that?'

'If I get within ten yards of him, I keep wanting to throttle him.'

Wurzel began to sweep the floor ineffectually – and the toes of the Hulk's minute D.M.s.

'And another thing –'

'Yeah?'

'Why don't you drop off an' all?'

The atmosphere on the Inter-City Express was chilly as Boxer and Charlotte attempted to ignore each other completely. Then the train hit some points, shuddered and her rucksack hurtled out of the rack. Reacting quickly, Boxer saw it coming, tried to stop it, hit the table with his knees as he rose – and shot Charlotte's coke all over his magazines and her coat.

'Oh, no!' she yelled.

'Sorry.'

'I should think you are.'

'Your rucksack nearly hit you.'

'Well – it didn't.'

'I was only trying to help,' said Boxer indignantly.

'My coat's ruined!'

'You should be thankin' me.'

'What for? Drowning me with coke?'

'At least I deflected your rucksack – saved you a right bang on the head.'

'Oh, don't be stupid.'

Angrily Charlotte rose to her feet and began to make her way towards the toilet.

When she returned, they both exchanged uncomfortable looks. Then as Charlotte sat down, she saw that Boxer's magazines were saturated with coke.

'I'm sorry about your magazines,' she said, still truculently.

'No sweat – you said they were a load of old rubbish anyway, didn't you?'

'I did say I was sorry.'

Suddenly they both knew the heat had gone out of their mutual dislike.

'Name's Billy Reed. Boxer to me mates.'

'I'm Charlotte Masters. Charlie.'

'Blimey. Charlie?' Boxer gave her a big cheeky grin and she smiled warily.

'Before you say it – don't bother. It's been said – dozens of times.'

'So, how far you going?'

'Next station.'

'Snap.'

There was a short silence. Then she said:

'You been abroad?'

'Why?'

'You've got a tan.'

'Can't think why. Where I was, you spend most of your time keeping out of it.'

'Where was that then?'

'Kuwait.'

'That can't be bad.' She looked envious.

'If bein' stuck on a building site in the middle of the desert turns you on. My dad works there – just spent me summer holidays with 'em.'

'That's nice.'

'Hallo – we're comin' in. Now do you want a hand with that bag?'

The train was slowing down, rattling into the station.

'I don't, thanks.'

'Independent, aren't we?'

'Yes.'

She gave him a long, hard look and then began to struggle with the rack. Boxer left her to it and, after a fashion, she managed. Then the train came to a halt and they both struggled out on to the platform. There, Boxer tried again:

'Can't I carry that for you?'

'No, thanks.'

As they walked down the length of the platform, Boxer said cheerfully:

'Do you like football?'

'You bet.'

Boxer glanced at her in surprise and she caught the look.

'Shouldn't I?'

'No,' he said hastily. 'No reason. Do you ever get down to United then?'

'United?' she replied scornfully. 'Do me a favour.'

'I thought you said you was into football.'

'I *am* into football.'

Boxer digested her comments as they handed in their tickets. As they passed through the barrier, he said:

'So, who's your football team, then?'

'The only one round here. Town, of course.'

'Dunmore Town?' said Boxer with disgust. 'They're nothing – they've been livin' in our shadow for years.'

'Well, not for much longer, eh?'

Now they were in the forecourt of the station, walking towards the taxi-rank.

'What's that supposed to mean?' asked Boxer aggressively.

'Don't you know?'

'Don't I know what?'

'Course, you've been away, haven't you?'

'So?' He stopped by the taxi-rank, staring at her in bafflement. 'What are you on about?'

'Well –'

'Hi, Charlie.'

Boxer whipped round to see a boy of his own age and build standing smiling at Charlotte.

'Hi, Jud.'

'Good trip?'

'Brilliant – had some coke thrown over me – but apart from that it was all right. Jud Prior meet Boxer Reed.'

Boxer and Jud nodded at each other. Both sensed rivalry, both were weighing each other up.

'Boxer's a United fan,' said Charlotte.

'In that case you have my deepest sympathy.'

'There's only one team round here these days,' replied Boxer.

'That's very true,' said Jud and laughed. Charlotte joined in his laughter and Boxer sensed that he was being excluded from a private joke.

'You taking a taxi?' asked Boxer, wondering if he should suggest sharing it with them. But Jud quietly said:

'Taxi's for nobs. We're taking the bus.' A few seconds later, a bus drew up and they both clambered on board. As the bus began to move away, Charlotte waved at Boxer through the window.

'Bye.'

He waved back as casually as possible and then shrugged, thinking, that's that, then. But what puzzled him was the way they had laughed. What did they know that he didn't?

When he arrived back in Mac's house, Boxer found a pile of letters in the hall. None of them were for him and he wondered how long they had been lying around – and why? Boxer lodged with Mac and his wife while his parents were abroad. Mac was the manager of Dunmore United.

Boxer walked into the living room.

'Mac? Elaine?' he said softly, but the house was obviously deserted. Then he saw something on the mantelpiece, propped up against a photograph of Mac, Elaine and the new baby. It was a letter addressed to himself.

Suddenly the doorbell rang and as Boxer opened the door, Rasputin hurried inside. He looked extremely agitated.

'Close the door,' he hissed.

'What's goin' –'

'I said – close the door!'

Mystified, Boxer did as he was told. Then the doorbell rang again.

'Hang on,' said Rasputin.

'What?'

'If he asks for me – I just left.' With this mysterious statement, Rasputin hurried inside the living room. The doorbell rang again urgently. Boxer paused and then opened the door. On the steps stood a man in his early thirties.

'Yeah?'

'Geoff Lythgoe, *Evening Sentinel*. Can I speak to Rasputin Jones?'

'He just left,' said Boxer unconvincingly.

Lythgoe smiled sardonically. 'I saw him come in here – not thirty seconds ago.'

'Sure,' said Boxer. 'He came in all right. Then he left.'

'There's nobody come out through this door, mate.' He was obviously getting riled.

'He went out the back.'

'I see.' Lythgoe stared at him. 'He came straight in the front – and straight out the back.'

'Funny, wasn't it?'

'Hilarious. Tell you another funny thing.'

'Yeah?'

'His car's still out there.'

'He fancied a bit of a walk,' said Boxer, trying to close the front door.

'Wait a minute.' Lythgoe put his foot in the door. 'When Mr Jones gets back from his walk –'

'Yeah?'

'Or gets out from under the bed, I want you to give him a message for me, son.'

'What's that?'

'Tell him he's got to face the press sooner or later – and if he's got any sense, he'll make it sooner. The people of this town have a right to know just what's happening to their football club. Right?'

'Right,' said Boxer.

When Boxer returned to Mac's living room, Rasputin gave him a round of slow, sarcastic applause.

'That was terrific. Now when I commit murder and need a reliable witness to give me a cast-iron alibi, I'll come straight to you.'

'What the 'ell do you expect when I don't know what's goin' on?' said Boxer indignantly. 'What *is* going on anyway?'

'It's simple enough really.'

'Is it?'

'What you've just witnessed, my son, is a first-class example of a member of the public bein' hounded by the press.'

'But what's all this about the club?'

'Haven't got time to tell you –'

'Look.'

'I *said* – I haven't got time. Isn't Mac back yet?'

'Where from?'

'Australia.'

'*What?*' Boxer looked at him, amazed.

'Didn't you know?'

'Of course I didn't.'

'Blimey,' said Rasputin pityingly. 'No one tells you nothin' – do they? He had this offer of a coaching job from one of the big Aussie clubs. It was only for a few weeks during the closed season so I let him go. Elaine and the baby went with him. Didn't they let you know?'

Boxer suddenly remembered the letter and he waved it at Rasputin. 'They left me this. I haven't had time to read it yet.'

'I see – well that should clear things up. Meanwhile – I've got a telephone call to make.'

'Be my guest.'

Rasputin picked up the phone and began to dial. Then he said, 'Dunmore Town? Put me through to the chairman, will you? Rasputin Jones speaking. Eh? What do you mean, he's not in? Or do you mean he's just not in to me? No – no message.' Rasputin banged down the telephone furiously. Suddenly, he realized that Boxer was standing in the doorway, looking worried.

'Rasputin –'

'Look – do me a favour. Have a quick shufti and make sure the coast is clear.'

Boxer grudgingly moved to the door. He opened it and looked out. 'Doesn't seem to be anybody about.'

'Good,' said Rasputin, moving out into the street. 'I'll see you then.'

'Hang on,' said Boxer indignantly.

'Well?'

'Can't you let me know what's going on?'

'Ask Mac when he gets back.'

'When's that?'

'Should have been yesterday. Perhaps he stopped off in Hong Kong and got himself shanghaied or something ... See you.' He hurried out into the street, looked around him furtively and then sprinted towards his car.

Boxer stared after him as Rasputin drove smartly away. Then he picked up Mac's letter again.

★

Next morning Boxer skidded his bike to a halt in amazement as he saw the roped-off forecourt of the Dunmore United Football Ground.

'Blimey.' He could hardly believe his eyes. Beyond some NO ENTRY signs he could see that the demolition of the ground was in active progress. Boxer parked his bike, ducked under a rope and walked over the debris-scattered forecourt. Unbelievingly, he made his way over the rubble to the door of the clubhouse and traced the outline where the sign used to be. Then he tried the door, only to find it locked.

For a moment Boxer stood there, completely bewildered, watching a lorry load of rubble coming out of the ground. Sticking out of its back was a sign which read: DUNMORE UNITED FOOTBALL CLUB LTD. Boxer stared at it, hypnotized, until he heard a shout.

'Oi!'

Boxer turned round abruptly and saw that a burly site foreman wearing a safety helmet was bearing down on him.

'Hoppit!'

'Hang on –'

'Look, son, I said hoppit.'

'Just tell me what's goin' on here.'

'What does it look like? The Lord Mayor's throwing a bit of a garden party and he's asked us to plant the lawn.'

'Blimey! But what's happening to the club?' asked Boxer desperately.

'You can read, can't you?'

'Yeah.'

'Then look over there.'

On the very edge of the site, Boxer could just make out a notice that read:

'Blimey.'

'You said that before. And I've told you to hoppit before. And if I have to tell you again –' He made a threatening step towards Boxer, who suddenly grabbed his bike, swung into the saddle and pedalled furiously away.

In Outer Space, Cassidy beckoned Wurzel over to him.

'Yeah?'

'Don't look now –'

'Eh?'

'But that boy over there in the corner.'

'Oh, him. You mean Pacman.'

'Pacman?'

'That's what they call him. Amazin' though, innit? The nicknames some kids put up with.'

'Never mind about that,' said Cassidy sharply. 'Just keep an eye on him, will you?'

'Why, Mr Cassidy?'

'I'll tell you why, Glossop. Because he's been on that machine ever since he came in here.'

'So?'

'And I've yet to see him put any more money into it.'

'You think he's found a way of getting a free game, Mr Cassidy?'

'I'm certain of it,' said Cassidy.

Wurzel picked up his brush. 'Right – just leave it to me, Mr Cassidy. It's not for nothin' my old man's a copper.'

'Get to it.'

'Sir.'

Wurzel started a wide sweep which eventually positioned him by the machine Pacman was playing, watched by Jenny and Hulk. Turning, he winked furtively at Cassidy, who nodded impatiently, his lips a thin, disapproving line. Then the telephone in the office rang and Cassidy stomped off to answer it.

Jenny stared at Wurzel suspiciously. 'What are you up to?'

'Surveillance job, innit,' he replied.

'What?'

'For my friend and benefactor, Mr Cassidy himself. He's got it into his tiny mind that Pacman here keeps gettin' himself free games on the machines.'

'He does.'

'Oh yeah?'

'Because he's so good – he wins all the time. That's why we all call him Pacman, stupid.'

'I know that, and you know that. But guess who doesn't?'

'Who?'

'Mr C.'

'So, tell him.'

'And ruin everythin'?'

'How do you mean?'

'Look – I'm not stupid. If you was workin' here in your spare time and you have a choice between sweepin' up all the time and doin' surveillance on old Pac here – which would you rather be doin'?'

'Oh – it's a skive, is it?'

'Doin' what I was told. With a bit of imagination I can keep this surveillance goin' until the end of the school holidays.'

'Don't look now.'

'What?'

'But I think he wants you – your friend and benefactor.'

Wearily, Wurzel walked back to Cassidy. 'Yes, Mr Cassidy?'

'One further point, Glossop,' he said in a measured voice. 'Just because I asked you to keep an eye on that boy, I would be really upset if you let it interfere with your more pressing duties.'

'Of course not, Mr Cassidy.'

'I would get very shirty if it did.'

'I'm sure you would, Mr Cassidy.'

As Boxer came in, Cassidy disappeared back into his office and Wurzel swept his way over. Jenny, delighted to see Boxer, also hurried up to him.

'Guess who?' said Boxer amiably.

'Boxer!' yelled Jenny, and Wurzel said, 'How are you, mate?'

'All right. Here – I've just been down the ground and they're ripping the place to pieces. What the hell's goin' on?'

'You tell us,' replied Wurzel gloomily.

'You mean you don't know?'

'Nobody seems to know,' said Jenny. 'Look, let's grab some coffee and we'll tell you what we do know.'

'Which ain't much,' put in Wurzel helpfully.

In the Outer Space coffee bar, Jenny and Wurzel began to hold forth to a fascinated Boxer.

'It all started with these rumours, right?' began Wurzel.

''Bout a week after you left,' said Jenny.

'What rumours?'

'About the club bein' in dead financial trouble.' Wurzel's voice was hoarse with dramatic emotion.

'What's new?'

'It was bad – so they said.' Jenny was less dramatic, more

forceful. 'This time there was even talk about the club goin' out of business altogether – if extra money couldn't be found.'

'So?'

'Well,' Wurzel spoke softly, 'Rasputin had the press and the telly round, right? And he says – yeah, there's a bit of a cash flow problem – like we could just do with half a million to get us off the hook. But no sweat, 'cos he had this plan for gettin' United out of the red, once and for all.'

'What was that?'

'And he'd be announcing the details within a couple of weeks. But so far we've heard nothin'.'

'Well, his plan couldn't have been to sell the site to a flamin' supermarket, could it?' said Boxer impatiently.

'We don't know,' replied Wurzel. 'The next thing that happens is that suddenly the ground's closed and the bull-dozers are movin' in.'

'But he can't just sell off the place,' said Boxer.

'Why not?' asked Jenny. 'He practically owns it, lock, stock and barrel. I suppose, in the end, a football club's just a business like anything else.'

'Which you can sell off if you want to,' put in Wurzel cynically. ''Specially if you're broke and someone's offering you a fat profit.'

'Mac wouldn't stand for it,' said Boxer firmly.

'He's only the manager.'

'Mac was in Australia when it happened,' snapped Jenny.

'Yeah,' said Wurzel. 'Makes you think, doesn't it?'

'What about?'

'About Rasputin agreein' to let him go in the first place – almost as if he wanted him out of the way.'

''Allo, 'allo, 'allo,' rasped a familiar voice. 'Summit conference?' Cassidy stood there, frowning.

'Just havin' me coffee break,' said Wurzel guiltily.

'We don't have coffee breaks, Glossop. Get back to work at once.'

'When you've got to go – you've got to go,' said Wurzel gloomily. 'See you lot later.' He departed, followed by Cassidy.

'Where's the rest of the mob, then?' Boxer asked Jenny.

'Gerry's in the Isle of Wight.'

'Holiday?'

'Permanently. His dad got a job there. Gonk's at Manchester United.'

'So, he finally signed pro?'

'Seemed a bit daft not to, especially when he got such rotten O-levels. It was pretty obvious he wasn't going to make it as a vet.'

'Blimey,' said Boxer.

'What's up?'

'Well, you turn your back for a couple of months and all of a sudden the entire universe falls apart.'

'It's not as bad as all that, Boxer.'

'Isn't it?'

Mac Murphy put the telephone down and walked into his living room. Suitcases were still lying around unpacked and Elaine came in from the kitchen with a baby's bottle.

'Did you get Rasputin?'

'No reply. I'd best get down there and find out what's going on.'

'I hope that man knows what he's doing, Mac.'

'He usually does – at least in my experience. Why?'

'I was just expecting that by the time we got back it would all be sorted out. Now, from what I gather, nothing's been sorted out at all.'

'Let's just see what he says, shall we?'

There was a sudden commotion from the hall and Boxer, Wurzel, Jenny, Pacman and Hulk hurtled in.

'Hi!'

'Boxer!' Elaine gave him an enormous hug. 'You're looking great.'

'Thanks. You've looking pretty good yourself.'

'So where is it then?' said Mac brusquely.

'What?' asked Boxer guardedly.

'The camel you promised to bring back for the baby.'

'Yeah – well I got it as far as the airport. Then it sort of took the hump.'

There were groans all round.

'How is the baby?' asked Boxer.

'Nothing's changed,' said Elaine ruefully. 'He still sleeps all day, cries all night.'

'So what's up then, Mac?' The note of alarm was clear in Boxer's voice.

'How do you mean?'

'Down at United.'

'Ask me again. After I've talked to Rasputin.'

'You mean you don't know what's goin' on at your own club?' asked the Hulk unpleasantly.

'No, that's not what I mean. And just for the record – who are you?'

'You can call me Hulk. Everybody else does.'

'The Hulk? You mean when you get mad you start splitting your shirts?'

'Somethin' like that.' The Hulk gave a sheepish grin.

Mac turned to Elaine. 'See you later.'

'Right.'

When he had gone, she turned to the expectant crowd.

'Now don't start on me. He's the boss – when it comes to United, anyway.'

'Surely you can tell us one thing,' pleaded Jenny.

'Which is –?'

'Have United gone bust?'

Elaine frowned. Then she answered reluctantly, 'I suppose it would be true to say they have. Yes.'

As the faces fell around her, she added quickly, 'On the other hand, perhaps things had to get worse before they get better.'

'What sort of answer's that?' said Pacman.

'Well,' said Elaine firmly, 'it's the only answer you're going to get for the present – until Mac says otherwise.' She picked up the baby's feeding bottle. 'And now, if you'll excuse me, I do have rather more important things to see to – more important than Dunmore United Football Club, anyway.'

They all looked at her in amazement.

'What could be more important than Dunmore United?' asked the Hulk.

'So what's happening?' Mac faced Rasputin squarely across his desk.

'Not a lot, mate,' replied Rasputin grimly.

'Come again?'

'Not a lot.'

Mac frowned. 'Just what are you trying to tell me, Mr Chairman? There's been a hitch?'

Rasputin laughed hollowly. 'You sound a bit like that stranded American astronaut when he was on his way back from the moon and found out his spaceship was wonky. We have a problem. Yes – well, I'd say that just about sums up our position. We do have a problem.'

'Look, when I left for Australia it was all cut and dried. We merged with Dunmore Town and played all our matches on their ground. Has this gone wrong?'

'No, we just have a problem about it.'

'Will you stop saying that?'

'I can't say it any other way, Mac.'

'You mean you sold the ground before you'd actually finalized the deal?'

'I had no choice, did I?'

'What!' Mac looked as if he was going to leap up and strike him.

Rasputin continued hurriedly, 'Look, Mac – as far as the supermarket was concerned, it was an either/or situation. They wanted to get in quickly before Sainsbury's or some-body else beat 'em to it and they had another town centre site lined up. So if they hadn't got the immediate go-ahead from us they'd have gone for that, wouldn't they? And we needed the money. Desperately.'

'But you still hadn't got a deal, had you?' pursued Mac with infinite patience.

'Oh yes, we have a deal. What do you take me for – stupid or something? We had the papers ready – everything. All we want are the signatures and we're in business.'

'So what's the problem?' Mac's voice was tinged with steely patience, as if he were talking to an imbecile who nevertheless had vital information stored in a cavernous mind.

'The problem is,' said Rasputin finally, 'that we haven't got the sigs. And that means we can't make any announce-ment, can we?'

'What happens if you don't manage to get those signa-tures?'

'We'll get 'em.'

'But if we don't . . .'

'If we don't, the problem's solved, mate.'

'How?' asked Mac icily.

'Well, let's face it, there isn't going to be a United to worry about any more, is there?'

'Been keeping busy, Glossop?' Cassidy had crept up behind Wurzel who, at the sound of his voice, leapt to his broom like a demented ferret.

'Never stopped once, Mr Cassidy.'

'Until just now?'

'Just snatchin' a well-earned breather.'

'Right – this way.'

Miserably, Wurzel followed Cassidy to the kitchen behind the Outer Space coffee bar. He paused by a large sink. It was full of dirty pots and pans.

'Now then, Glossop,' said Cassidy cheerfully, 'I don't know whether you've ever come across one of these before?'

'What?'

'It's called a sink.'

'Oh, yes.'

'Now, the operation is *fairly* simple, but I will explain it in detail.'

'Thank you, Mr Cassidy.'

'In fact – I'd go so far as to say that it's even within your own limited capabilities. You see – we turn the water on here – so. We now add soap, and after that you require elbow grease.'

'Oh, yeah?' Wurzel looked unhappily at the dirty sink.

'So, since you've now presumably had your well-earned breather, let's get on with it, shall we?'

''Ang on a minute, Mr Cassidy. Aren't you forgetting something?' asked Wurzel with mounting desperation.

'Yes?'

'When I agreed to join your little team here, nobody said nothing about me being lumbered with washin' up.'

'Oh dear,' said Cassidy, all mock concern, 'didn't they?'

'No.'

'Well, you see, when I agreed to form this little team, Glossop, nobody said nothing to me about being lumbered with somebody like you. So learn to live with it, Glossop.'

'Right, Mr C. Only before I do, there's just one thing I ought to mention.'

'And what's that?' Cassidy smiled ferociously.

'Well, it's this thing I 'ave, you see.'

'What thing?' His voice was like granite.

'About pots. You know Yuri Geller?'

'Yes.'

'And whenever he gets hold of spoons they start bendin'?'

'Yes.'

'With me it's pots.'

'Is it?'

'Whenever I get 'old of pots – 'specially dirty pots – they just seem to start comin' apart right in me 'ands!'

'Do they now?'

'In fact, my mum reckons it's a sign. You know – that I just wasn't destined to be one of the great washers-up of life.'

'No sweat, Glossop. As far as breakages are concerned, the usual arrangement will, of course, prevail.'

'What's the usual arrangement, Mr Cassidy?'

'Appropriate deductions for all breakages will be made at the end of the week.'

'Blimey.'

'Yes – and now I must get on. I've really enjoyed our conversation, Glossop. I do hope the feeling is reciprocal.'

'Eh?'

'Au revoir.' Cassidy hurried out, looking delighted with his victory, while Wurzel glared down at the cluttered sink.

Rasputin banged down the phone angrily. 'I heard him,' he said.

'Heard what?' asked Mac.

'Heard him telling his secretary he wasn't there.'

'Ronnie Wright?'

'The very man.'

'What now?'

'If the mountain won't come to Mahomet, then Mahomet is goin' to have to go to the flamin' mountain, isn't he?' Rasputin rose majestically to his feet and put on his coat. 'Not that Ronnie Wright is much of a mountain, mind you. More of a small molehill which is goin' to get well and truly flattened when I catch up with it.'

'And just where,' said Mac slowly, 'does that leave me?'

'How do you mean?'

'Well, in case you hadn't noticed, somebody seems to have driven a bulldozer through what used to be my office. So what am I supposed to do? Work from home?'

'If you like.'

'Thanks. That'll be very inconvenient with the baby.'

'Why don't you make yourself at home here? Use Derek Cassidy's desk – he won't mind. And if he does, that's just his hard luck, isn't it? So I'll see you later.'

'O.K. And the very best of luck.'

'I might need it.'

Rasputin hurried out and Mac went over to Cassidy's desk. He tried out the chair and put his feet up on the desk. It was going to be a waiting game, with the entire future of Dunmore United at stake. Suddenly Mac fervently wished himself back in Australia. Then there was a thunderous knock on the door and a good deal of stifled whispering.

'Yes?' said Mac wearily.

Boxer, Jenny, Pacman, Hulk and Wurzel all came trailing into the office looking as if the bottom had dropped out of the world. Wurzel, who was nearest to him, exuded a strong, sweet smell.

'Blimey,' said Mac. 'You had a bath?'

'No.'

'Then what can I smell? I thought you'd bathed with the lilies of the field.'

'Washing-up liquid,' said Wurzel gloomily. 'I'm just the char round here.'

'Very suitable.'

'Thanks.'

'What's happening, Mac?' asked Jenny impatiently.

'Is this a delegation?'

'We just want to know what happens to United,' she insisted.

'What makes you think I know?'

'If you don't,' said Boxer, 'who does?'

'Please, Mac,' pleaded Jenny. 'Please tell us.'

'So that you lot can blab it all over town?'

'You do realize you're talking to the Dunmore United Junior Supporters' Club, Mac?' said Wurzel angrily.

'And that's meant to reassure me? Because let me tell you, son, it doesn't. Anything but.'

'Mac, we'll all go round the bend if we don't find out something soon.' Boxer's voice was so desperate that Mac hesitated, thought and then said:

'All right, but I'm telling you, if one word of what I say gets out, I'll have your guts for garters.'

'Right,' they all chorused.

'So, who's got the first question?'

'How can a team that's just been promoted be in deep financial trouble?' asked Boxer.

'For that very reason, son.' Mac's voice was very grim. 'It's a fact of life in football that the higher you climb the more it costs to stay up there. So at the end of the day we might have a trophy on the sideboard, but we've also come out of it with one hell of an overdraft at the bank.'

'So what's new about that?' asked the ever-gracious Pacman.

'What's new about it is that this time Rasputin Jones didn't feel he could just stick his hand in his pocket and find the money to bail us out. Because this time he just didn't have that kind of money in his pocket.'

There was a short silence. Then Boxer said, 'So what are you tellin' us, Mac? That United have gone bust?'

'What I'm tellin' you, Boxer, is that we were up to our eyeballs in debt. And that money had to be found from somewhere.'

The Hulk cleared his throat. 'And Rasputin found it by sellin' off our pitch to a supermarket.'

Mac gave him a long, cool look. 'Wrong, son.'

'Then, what?'

'He found it by selling off *his* pitch to a supermarket.'

'But you can't have a football club without a ground,' worried Boxer. Mac gave him an impatient glance.

'Look, do you think Rasputin is stupid?'

'He hasn't been in the past,' said Boxer.

'And he's not now. He had a ground lined up.'

'Which ground?' asked Pacman.

'Dunmore Town,' replied Mac, conscious that he was

about to cause a storm. He did and there were mixed reactions of astonishment and horror all round.

'They'd never sell their ground, Mac,' put in Boxer.

'That wasn't the idea.'

'Then –'

'The plan was a merger of the two clubs into one.'

There were more horrified expressions as Hulk put everyone's thoughts into words when he said:

'You must be jokin'!'

'No,' said Mac calmly.

'A merger with Town?' continued the Hulk. 'Their supporters aren't human. It's a well-known fact, that is.'

'I see – whereas you and the rest of the United fans are a real set of choirboys, right? In fact, aren't you all famous throughout the League for having better manners than Barbara Cartland? Anyway, as a matter of fact, a merging of clubs makes all sorts of sense for all sorts of reasons. Not just for us – but for half the clubs in the Football League. There can't be many things more stupid in this day and age than having two clubs in the same area that are both strapped for cash. Both fighting each other to death for the same dwindling audience. By putting the two clubs together we double the gate, halve the running costs and, with any luck, after selling one of the grounds, end up with plenty of money in the kitty to strengthen the playing staff.'

They all gazed at him uncertainly after his long speech and then Boxer said, 'So, we're O.K. then. No problem?'

'Unfortunately it's not as simple as that.'

'Why?' asked Jenny.

'There's a snag.'

'How do you mean?' Pacman too was becoming increasingly uneasy.

32

'It seems there's a bit of a hiccough at the Town end of things.'

'You mean the deal might not go through after all?' The alarm grew in Boxer's voice.

'It's possible.'

'But the ground's already been sold.'

'And flattened,' put in the Hulk.

'I know.'

'So?' said Jenny grimly.

'So you wanted to know what the score was. That's it.'

Rasputin's Rolls speeded out of the forecourt of the Town ground and skidded to a halt outside the club offices. Quickly, Rasputin got out of the car, locked it and was suddenly aware of a presence.

Watching him menacingly was Mugsy Moran, twelve years old, scruffy, chunky and baby-faced. There was calculation in his little blue eyes as he said to Rasputin, 'Want it watchin' for you, Mister?'

'Pardon?' Rasputin looked down at Mugsy as if he was something unpleasant on the road.

'Your car,' Mugsy repeated. 'You want it watchin'?'

'Why? What were you expectin' it to do? Sit up on its back legs and play "God Save the Queen"?'

But Mugsy didn't see the joke.

'Things happen sometimes to cars left round here.'

Rasputin looked at him knowingly. 'Oh yeah? What kind of things?'

'Nasty things. Like somebody might let your tyres down – or nick your hub-caps.'

'Oh, I see.'

'It wouldn't be nice. Not with a posh motor like yours.'

'Whereas it would be nicer if I was to ask you to keep an eye on it for me while I was in there. Safer like.'

'That's it, mister. You're quite right.'

'What's this goin' to cost me then? This protection you're offerin'?'

'Fifty pence.'

'Fifty pence, eh? Cheap at the price, I'd say. Special offer is it today?'

'Yeah,' Mugsy grinned horribly, thinking he'd netted a customer.

Rasputin gave him a dangerously sweet smile. 'So what's your name? Father Christmas?'

'Me mates call me Mugsy.'

'What's your second name – Malone?'

'Moran,' he corrected.

'And you live round here, do you, Mugsy?'

'Thirty-five, Railway Terrace.'

'That's good.'

'Why?' The first dawning of suspicion appeared on Mugsy's little face.

'Well,' said Rasputin softly, 'we'll know where to come lookin' for you, then. Won't we?'

'What do you mean?'

'Me and the local fuzz.'

'What?' Fury appeared on Mugsy's delinquent features. He knew that he had been trapped.

'Now,' said Rasputin, leaning over him. 'If when I get back anybody has so much as laid one dirty little finger on my motor here, I'll shop you. Message received and understood?'

Mugsy glared up at Rasputin sullenly.

'Now you want some advice?'

Mugsy said nothing but continued to glare.

34

'When I was half your age, son, I was running a lucrative little protection racket of my own down at the local car park. So my advice, Mugsy old bean, is to give it up. Why don't you find something more in your line? Like dog-watchin' or baby-sittin'.'

With this last word, Rasputin turned on his heel and walked into the clubhouse. When he had disappeared, Jud, the boy Boxer had met at the station with Charlotte, appeared with a thickset mate called Blocker. They went up to the still smarting Mugsy and said, 'All seemed to go 'orribly wrong, didn't it, Mugs?'

'How's your grandmother?' asked Ronnie Wright of Charlotte Masters.

'You know Gran – she does her crying in private.'

'Terrible shock for her, him dying so sudden like that.'

'Yes, it's been awful.'

'You'll find everything in that rolltop desk over there.'

Charlotte walked slowly towards it and with some hesitation opened up the top. Inside were piles of photographs, medals, badges and other sporting bits and pieces. Quietly, she scooped them up and began to put them in the two large carrier bags she had brought in with her.

'He was quite a man – we'll miss him.'

'So will we, Mr Wright,' said Charlotte, continuing to clear the desk as quickly as she could. Then she heard him mutter, 'Blimey.'

'What's the matter?'

He turned to her, frantically gesticulating. 'Shhhh!'

Then she heard a terrific commotion outside, with the voice of Beryl, Ronnie's secretary, raised in protest.

'I've told you, he's not here.'

'Well, look,' said an irate man's voice, 'I'll tell you what, let's just find out, shall we?'

'Now hang on a minute.'

'What are you doing?' hissed Charlotte as Ronnie tried to lock the door silently. Unfortunately, he failed and the lock clicked loudly.

'Damn.'

'Who is it?'

'Rasputin Jones – United's chairman. Shh,' he hissed.

Through the door, Charlotte heard Rasputin say, 'Hallo in there, Ronnie. Are you receivin' me? Over.'

'Look,' said Beryl in a muffled voice, 'there's nobody in there.'

To her mounting unease, Charlotte heard Rasputin say, 'Course not. In fact that was the Ghost of Christmas Past I just heard snap the lock on.'

Ronnie froze, half-crouched beside the door as he listened to Rasputin.

'Right then. A message for your beloved chairman when he comes in – or should I say out from under the boardroom table. Tell him to be in touch. Soon. Because the longer this rubbish goes on, the worse my temper's goin' to get. And when I'm in a really bad temper I'm not very nice to know. In fact I have been known to get quite frighteningly violent. All right?'

They heard him move away and slam the door of the outer office.

'Phew,' said Ronnie, straightening up. 'That was close.'

When Rasputin emerged, furious, from the clubhouse, he saw Jud, Mugsy and Blocker standing in a group, staring at his Rolls. Pointedly taking a good look around his car, Rasputin got in. As he drove off he wound down the window and, with a beatific smile, said to Mugsy, 'Not a mark on it. Very wise, my son.'

He drove off, but did not go very far. A few streets later, he pulled in and switched off the engine. Checking his watch, he took out one of his thin cigars. Slowly and carefully he lit up.

Charlotte joined Jud, Blocker and Mugsy outside the club.

'Carry your bags, love?'

'Be careful then, Jud – they're all Grand-dad's things.'

'Course I will.'

As they set off, Mugsy asked, 'What do you think was goin' on then?'

'Dunno,' replied Charlotte. 'The whole thing was so weird.'

'Maybe Rasputin was after a job on the board – now that United's gone bust on him,' said Blocker.

'Well, he was wastin' his time,' Charlotte assured him. 'Ronnie Wright wouldn't even talk to him. Where we goin', anyway?'

'Into town,' said Jud.

'Into town where?'

'To this new place I found,' said Jud with a sly, mysterious air. 'In fact – I've got this bit of Dunmore Town Football Club business on. Haven't I, lads?'

They nodded obligingly.

'What business?' asked Charlotte.

'You'll see. Come on, Peg Leg – best foot forward, eh?'

In Outer Space, Mac was looking for Boxer. Spotting him, he hurried over.

'Oi.'

'Yes, Mac?'

'Quick word in the office?'

'Sure.'

As they went off to Rasputin's inner sanctum, Charlotte came in with her retinue.

'This place?' She looked around her in disbelief.

'Why not?' grinned Jud.

'This is where all the United fans hang out.'

'Don't let that put you off, love.'

Jud marched boldly through the rows of machines, followed less enthusiastically by the others. Several kids eyed his Town scarf with distaste, but this had no effect on Jud as he led his followers through to the coffee bar.

'Saudi Arabia?' said Boxer in surprise as he sat on the edge of Rasputin's desk.

'Elaine took the call about half an hour ago,' said Mac.

'Who was callin'?'

'Your dad.'

His surprise gradually turned to alarm. 'Nothin' wrong?'

'Shouldn't think so.'

'Why?'

'Well, if there was he'd have said so.'

'What *did* he say?'

'Not a lot – just that he wanted a word with you personally. Said he'd ring you back at seven tonight our time.'

'Oh, thanks.' Boxer rose to his feet.

'Hey.'

He paused. 'Yeah?'

'Stop worrying.'

'Easier said than done. I mean it's bound to be important, isn't it? Or he wouldn't ring me from halfway round the world.'

*

'What bit of business have you got on here, Jud?' asked Charlotte, sitting in the coffee bar of Outer Space, sipping a coke.

'Recruitin' business, Charlie.'

'What are you on about?'

'Well, it looks as if United have gone kaput, don't it?'

'So?'

'Then we've got a golden opportunity to recruit a few fans for Town.'

'You must be off your nut.'

'Why?' He looked instantly aggrieved.

'You'll never get United fans supportin' Town.'

Blocker intervened. 'Who else are they gonna support if there's no United any more?'

'They'll go out of town – follow one of the big clubs.'

'Yeah?' said Mugsy. 'They couldn't afford the train fares.'

'I'm still sure they won't follow Town.'

'Show her the poster, Blocker,' said Jud triumphantly.

Blocker grinned and produced a poster from his jerkin. 'Feast your eyes on this, darlin'.'

It read:

GO TO TOWN!
THIS SEASON FOLLOW
A REAL FOOTBALL TEAM:
DUNMORE TOWN – YOUR ONLY
LOCAL TEAM

Charlotte stared at the poster, shaking her head. 'You aren't seriously thinking of sticking that thing up in here, are you?'

'Why not? It's a free country, isn't it?'

'You know why not,' she persisted. 'If any of this lot in

here catch sight of that you'll have World War Three in a few minutes.'

Jud shrugged. 'Just tryin' to cheer 'em up a bit, Charlie. Make 'em realize there's still a football team in town.'

'Rubbish. You're not trying to cheer 'em up,' she said bitterly. 'You're just tryin' to stir it. And if you think I'm goin' to stop here and watch you do it, you've got another think comin'.'

'You chicken?' asked Blocker.

'No, I'm not chicken,' she replied angrily. 'I'm just not stupid like you are.'

Pacman and Hulk, seeing the arrival of the Town fans, had rushed to find Boxer. But he didn't seem that interested.

'So they're Town fans,' he said. 'So what?' Boxer's thoughts were literally miles away in Saudi Arabia.

'What are they doin' here then?' urged Pacman.

'Maybe they're space-invader nuts – like you.'

'Aren't you bothered?' asked the Hulk in a voice of horror.

'Course not.'

'Why?'

'Because – between you and me – I've got more important things on me mind. Know what I mean?'

'But they're here to cause trouble,' moaned Hulk.

'You don't know that.'

'Course, if they want it they can have it.' Hulk's voice became menacing.

The others nodded, gazing excitedly at Boxer who ignored them. Instead, he looked pityingly at Hulk. 'You know – you frighten me.'

'You!' The Hulk looked amazed.

'Funny, isn't it?' said Boxer. 'It must be your mind.'

A few feet away, in the coffee bar, Charlotte was having a blazing row with Jud.

'Put that poster away.'

'Why?'

'Because I said so.'

'So who do you think you are all of a sudden – Maggie Thatcher?'

'All right, Jud.' Charlotte's voice had a final note to it.

'What's all right?'

'I'm just warning you, Jud. If you don't put that thing away and there's a punch-up in here, I'll never speak to you again.'

'Yeah?'

'I mean it.'

Jud looked at her and realized she meant what she said. He turned to Blocker. 'All right, put it away.'

'Just 'cos she says so?'

'No –'

'Well, then –'

'Because I said so.'

Reluctantly Blocker put the poster inside his jerkin. Then Jud saw Boxer coming up to their table and he scowled. Charlie looked pleased.

'Hallo again,' said Boxer.

'Hi.'

'How you doin'?'

'All right.'

Boxer grinned at Jud, who seemed disconcerted.

'What are you doin' round this neck of the wood then?'

'Slummin' – what else?' said Blocker.

'Oh, great.' Boxer grinned dangerously at him. 'Well, enjoy yourselves.'

'We'll try,' said Jud. 'Won't be easy.'

'See you,' Boxer chuckled.

'Yeah,' said Charlotte.

Boxer disappeared and Jud commented, 'Friendly little soul, isn't he?'

'Not all that little,' replied Charlotte.

They looked at each other angrily.

Somewhat furtively, Ronnie Wright locked the door of the Dunmore Town F.C. offices and, looking nervously round the forecourt, hurried towards his car. But when he got in he found an unwelcome visitor in the front passenger seat.

'Guess who?' said Rasputin Jones jovially.

Ronnie looked as if he was going to pass out, but he tried unsuccessfully to bluster. 'What the 'ell's your game, then?'

'Oh, I've just invented it.'

'Yeah?'

'It's called "Find the Ronnie". Do you reckon it'll catch on?'

'How dare you get into my car like this.'

'Careless of you to leave it unlocked.'

'It wasn't unlocked. I locked it myself.'

'That's what they all say – after their car's been nicked.'

'I'll have the police on you.'

Rasputin leant over towards him and confided, 'Listen, Ronnie love, if I don't get some answers out of you it's not the police you're gonna need – it's a flamin' ambulance.'

'You don't frighten me, Jones.'

'No?'

Ronnie suddenly made a dive for the door, but Rasputin was too quick for him. He grabbed him in a vice-like grip and then stuck his face within an inch of Ronnie's.

'Now, Ronnie –'

'Let go.'

'Not till I get some answers. For instance – where were you about a week ago? Before you did your world-famous impression of the Invisible Man?'

'Look here –'

'Oh yeah, I know. We'd just shaken hands on the merger deal and told the solicitors to get on with the necessary paperwork. And I'd gone ahead with my own deal and sold my ground to the supermarket. So. You were sayin'?'

Looking like a scared mouse, Ronnie muttered, 'I'm sorry, the deal's off.'

'Off?' said Rasputin.

'Yeah – off.'

'Listen, mate – at this very moment there's a great big hole in the earth where my football ground used to be.'

Ronnie squirmed visibly. 'I'm – I'm really sorry about that, but there's nothing I can do.'

'No?' But before Rasputin could say anything else Ronnie tore himself loose, jumped out of the car and began to run down the road.

For a few seconds, Rasputin sat in the passenger seat in complete disbelief. Then he scrambled out in hot pursuit.

Charlotte was playing one of the machines when Boxer came up behind her.

'Winnin', are yer?'

Charlotte turned round and grinned arrogantly at him. 'Of course.'

Boxer watched her as she played on. Then he said, 'You know, when my old man was a kid they used to reckon that the sign of a misspent youth was bein' good at snooker. With our generation I reckon it'll be bein' good at these things.'

'You're right.' Then she lost. 'Oh, no . . .'

Boxer laughed casually. He was sure he was making the right approach. 'Not lookin' for bother, is he?'

'Who?'

'Your boyfriend.'

'Who says he's my boyfriend?'

'You sayin' he isn't?' said Boxer eagerly.

'He's just a good mate, that's all.'

'That's nice.'

'Why?'

'Why do you think?'

She looked at him suspiciously and Boxer grinned at her cheekily. Quickly Charlotte turned away, making a big production of looking in her purse for another coin.

'Fancy a two-hander, do you?'

She hesitated.

'Or wouldn't he like it?' goaded Boxer. 'That good mate of yours in there.'

Charlotte thought for a moment and then shrugged. 'Why not?'

But Jud, watching from the coffee-bar door, frowned aggressively.

Mac, with nothing to do and all the time in the world to worry, was reading a newspaper in Rasputin's office. Then there came a knock at the door.

'Yeah?'

Cassidy came in. 'Mac!' His voice took on a silky note. 'Back safely from Australia, then?'

'I'm afraid so, Derek.'

'Good. Er, was there something?'

'Sorry?'

'You're sitting at my desk.'

'Rasputin hasn't told you yet?'

'Told me what?'

'That for the moment I'll be using this office myself.'

'I see.'

'All right?'

'Well – it makes sense. I s'pose – under the circumstances – you'll be needing a desk.'

'This one's fine.'

'But it's *my* desk.' There was an edge to Cassidy's voice.

'Is it?'

'One would like to help out, of course.'

'Of course.'

'But at the same time my desk is in fairly constant use.'

'Don't you want to share?'

'Not really. Sorry.'

'Then will you tell him or shall I?'

'Who?' Cassidy was beginning to sound very worried.

'Rasputin. It was his idea.'

'Ah.'

'Is that O.K.?'

'Well, if it's for the good of the company . . .'

'It is.'

'Then I'd be delighted.'

'Very good of you to see it like that, Derek.'

'Not at all.'

Cassidy cleared his throat pompously. 'I do see it as part of my job to further the best interests of the company, wherever and whenever I can.' He glowed with self-righteousness.

'Do you know, I think that's one of the things wrong with this country today, Derek.'

'Oh yes?' He looked disconcerted now.

'There just ain't enough people like you around any more.'

Cassidy nodded, not sure how serious Mac was, but hoping for the best. In the end he became so confused that he left the room, leaving Mac smiling to himself. But then his thoughts returned to Dunmore United – or the lack of it.

Boxer had gone when Jud came out to claim Charlotte. He was in a dark mood when he said, 'Beat him, did you? Or wasn't that what mattered?'

'What do you mean?' she said, affecting not to be aware of his mood.

'What do you think I mean?'

Immediately Charlotte stopped bluffing. 'Look, Jud – let's get something straight, shall we?'

'Sure.'

'You're a good mate and I like you.'

'Thanks a million.'

'But then I like a lot of people.'

'Oh, yeah?'

'That doesn't make me their property though, does it? I'm not your girl any more than I'm anybody else's.'

'I see.'

'And remember, if you want us to carry on bein' good mates you'd better understand that.'

'Look, Charlie –'

But Charlotte was not prepared to discuss the situation any further and walked off angrily, leaving Jud feeling an idiot. This aggravated him even further. Blocker slid up beside him, grinning annoyingly. 'Lovers' tiff, eh?'

'You tryin' to be funny?'

'Who, me?' Blocker was still grinning but warily, knowing Jud had a temper – especially where Charlotte was concerned.

'Still got it on you, then?'

'Got what?'

'You know what. My poster.'

Blocker looked at him in surprise. 'I thought we'd decided not to bother, like. I mean – lookin' round this place does make me feel a bit like General Custer must have felt on his last stand.'

'Gimme.'

'Sure?'

'I'm sure.'

Reluctantly, Blocker gave him the poster.

'Now we'll show 'em,' said Jud grimly.

Rasputin tore into his office in a furious temper. Cassidy hurried out of his cubicle to try and intercept him.

'Mr Jones –'

'Yeah?' Rasputin looked at him as if he were a particularly slimy insect and Cassidy quailed for a moment. Desperately, he tried to rally.

'I wonder if I could have a word?'

'Not now, Derek.'

'It's about my desk, Mr Jones,' he said a little hysterically.

'Your desk?' Rasputin looked amazed. 'What's happened to it?'

'It's been taken over. By Mr Murphy.'

'So that's the major crisis, is it?'

'But, Mr Jones –'

'Yeah?'

'One's desk is one's desk.'

'You know, Derek, that's what I like about you.'

'Thank you, sir.'

'You have a very highly developed sense of priority.'

'Well, that's –'

'In fact, you'd have gone down a bomb with old Nero – the day they tried to burn down Rome right in the middle of his violin recital.'

'Er – Nero – Mr Jones?'

'Yeah. He went right on fiddlin'. And you'd have gone right on clappin' him. And to 'ell with the fact that the whole flamin' town was comin' down around your ears.'

'I'm sorry, Mr Jones,' said Cassidy. 'I just don't know what you mean.'

Rasputin spoke in measured tones. 'What I mean, Derek, is that when the whole flamin' town happens to be comin' down round my ears, I've got better things to worry about than your flippin' desk.' Without waiting for a reply, Rasputin thundered into his office and banged the door.

Cassidy stood, watching him go, his indignation rising. So he was hardly in the best of moods when he heard a voice say, 'Excuse me.'

'Yes,' Cassidy barked, staring balefully at Charlie.

'Er – there's a kid that comes in here. The others call him Boxer.'

'What about him?'

'You wouldn't happen to know where he was, would you?'

Cassidy rocked back on his heels, drew himself up – and gave her the full brunt of his temper. 'Don't you think I've got better things to do with my time?'

'Sorry, I –'

'I can't keep track of every yobbo that finds his way in here.' He turned away angrily and stomped back into his cubicle, muttering.

*

'At least you found him, anyway,' said Mac, trying to soothe the furious Rasputin.

Rasputin flung his coat violently on to the hook in his office, looking as if he could also hang up Ronnie Wright. Then he sat down violently behind his desk.

'I found out a bit more than that, mate. I found out what's been goin' on.'

'What the hell *is* going on?'

'A couple of weeks ago, Wright shook me warmly by the hand and told me this merger could go ahead on his say-so alone because he had as many shares in Dunmore Town as I have in United. So what he said went – right?'

'So?' said Mac, burning with impatience.

'So he was lyin'.'

'How?'

'Through his teeth. There's somebody else down at Town who owns nearly as many shares as he has.'

Mac paused and then spoke slowly, his spirits plummeting, 'Are you telling me that the other major shareholder doesn't want to go along with the scheme?'

'To be fair to Ronnie,' said Rasputin evasively, 'he did think it was only a formality. It seems this other shareholder's some old geezer who used to be a Big Noise down at Town, but hasn't been involved directly for years. He's always let Ronnie vote the shares as if they were his own.'

'So what's the problem?'

'The old geezer's snuffed it. Left us for that Great Big Football Club in the Sky.'

'Who got his shares?'

'His old girl – and she prefers to make up her own mind about things.'

'She against the merger?'

'According to Ronnie she's been a keen fan of Town

since time began and the last thing she wants to see is a merger.'

'Great,' said Mac bitterly. 'Where does that leave us?'

'Where do you think? Right up the flamin' creek – without a flamin' paddle.'

'Oi! What do you two think you're doin'?'

Molly, who ran the coffee bar in Outer Space, stood with her hands on her hips watching Jud and Blocker sticking their poster up on the wall.

'We're puttin' a poster up.'

'It's manners to ask.'

Jud turned to her, straight-faced and superficially penitent. 'Please, miss – can we put our poster up, please?'

'Let's have a look, first.'

Calmly, he showed it to her and waited, with Blocker, for the storm to break. It was not long in coming.

'You can't put that up in 'ere.' She was horrified.

'Why not? It's only a poster promotin' Dunmore Town.'

'That's the point.'

'I don't get yer.'

'There'll be a riot.'

Jud turned to Blocker. 'I dunno what she means, do you?'

'No,' he replied innocently.

'What about over there?' said Jud, pointing to another part of the wall. It was at this point that Wurzel, who was at the other end of the bar putting raspberry ripple on an ice-cream cornet, clearly announced:

'You 'eard her. What are you – stupid or something?'

Jud smiled sweetly at him. 'You talkin' to me?'

'Well, I'm not talking to the wall, am I?'

'Two cokes please, love,' said Jud, ignoring him.

Molly grudgingly sold him two cans.

'Have 'em and beat it,' she said while Wurzel continued, 'Course, if I *was* talkin' to a wall, I'd get more sense out of it.'

While he was talking Jud and Blocker both put their cans behind their backs and happily began to shake them.

'Seein' it's probably not half as thick.'

'I don't think I like his tone, Blocker,' said Jud.

'P'raps he needs to cool down a bit.'

With great speed, Blocker brought his can of coke from behind his back, ripped off the seal and directed it like a fire extinguisher at Wurzel, who was completely drenched. Molly gazed in mounting apprehension at his soaked figure while Jud and Blocker laughed uproariously.

But Wurzel still had the cornet in his hand and, as if in slow motion, he moved towards Blocker who continued to laugh. Neatly and very precisely, Wurzel jammed the cornet into his wide-open mouth. Blocker stopped laughing. There was a short, deadly silence, suddenly broken by Molly as she ran out, yelling for Cassidy, while Wurzel shouted, 'Assistance!'

Meanwhile Blocker slowly wiped the ice-cream from his face, grabbed a portion of sliced gâteau and threw it at Wurzel. Then, in answer to Wurzel's call, Pacman and Hulk arrived at the double. As he came in, Pacman caught a jet of coke from Jud's can full in the chest, but the Hulk put his head down and charged, butting Blocker in the stomach. He doubled up as Mugsy entered, only to be squirted in the eye by Wurzel with raspberry ripple.

As Boxer arrived on the scene he discovered the ice-cream- and coke-covered chaos, with Hulk attacking Blocker and Pacman fighting Mugsy.

'Knock it off, will you?' Boxer said to Jud.

'Who's gonna make me?' He put his hand in Boxer's face and pushed him away. At once this action put aside any ideas Boxer had of controlling the situation. Instead, he went piling into Jud, while Wurzel, thoroughly enjoying himself, ladled ice-cream from the fridge and hurled it in cricketball-sized shapes at the combatants. Then he got together a particularly juicy scoopful, coated it lovingly with raspberry sauce, dolloped it into his slippery, ice-cream-covered hand and threw it joyfully into the mêlée. The large globule hit Derek Cassidy full in the face as he came rushing into the coffee bar.

'Sorry, Mr Cassidy,' said Wurzel as Cassidy stood, frozen to the spot, slowly wiping ice-cream from his face.

Five minutes later, the ice-cream-splattered participants in the brawl were lined up in Rasputin's office while a secretly amused Mac and an enraged Cassidy stood in the background.

'Give me one good reason,' Rasputin was saying, 'why I shouldn't get on the blower and get you scruffos run in – all of you?' He glared at them, waiting in an almost perfect silence. Then he said, 'My – hasn't it gone quiet all of a sudden. Now it strikes me I haven't got the time right now to make statements, answer questions and sit around waiting for a court appearance, so we'll 'ave a collection instead – and I know you'll be generous.'

Rasputin took a large ash-tray from his desk and went along the line as if it was a collection plate. 'Dig,' he said, 'dig very deep.'

Slowly, they dropped coins in the ash-tray. When Rasputin came to Mugsy, he paused. 'Well – if it isn't my little mate, Mugsy – the Al Capone of the car parks. With all the rackets you got goin' on the side, I'm sure we can expect a generous contribution from you.' Mugsy dropped some coins in.

'And again.' He dropped some more.

'And a few more.' Mugsy reluctantly did as he was bid.

'Thank you so much.' Rasputin passed on to Wurzel who was waving a pound note.

'Got any change? All I've got is a quid.'

'That's all right, my old son, we're not proud.' And to Wurzel's horror he took his pound.

'Now then,' Rasputin turned on them all, 'get out – and I'm warnin' you that if I catch any one of you within five miles of this place – you'll be nicked. Now MOVE!'

Sullenly the kids shuffled out, while Cassidy said ingratiatingly, 'Could I just say on behalf of my staff and myself that this has been a judgment worthy of Solomon himself – under the circumstances.'

'Why, thank you, Derek.'

'And you won't forget the other small matter I mentioned.'

'Just leave it to me, eh?'

'Of course.'

He disappeared as Mac said, 'Must be a great feeling.'

'What?'

'Knowing you've got one fan, at least.'

Rasputin frowned. 'You've got to understand my position, Mac.'

'It's not a very productive one, is it?' he replied.

Boxer met Charlotte as he was coming through the door of Outer Space.

'What happened?' she asked.

'Not a lot. Except I lost a week's pocket money, thanks to you.'

'What?'

But he pushed past her, followed by the disgruntled trio of Wurzel, Pacman and Hulk. Sadly, she watched him go, surprised at his hostility. But when she turned round, Charlotte saw Jud standing in front of her.

Angrily, she burst out, 'I hope you're satisfied?'

'We've just had a collection,' he returned sarcastically, 'spare me the sermon.' He walked past her with Mugsy and Blocker, assuming she would follow. But she didn't.

'Aren't you comin' then?'

'No.'

'Why not?'

'Don't want to.'

'Please yourself.' He walked furiously away, the other two hurrying to keep up with him, only to discover Boxer pumping up the tyre of his bike on the pavement. With him were Wurzel, Pacman, Jenny and Hulk.

'Right,' said Wurzel, squaring up, intent on continuing hostilities.

'Come on, Wurzel – leave it, will you?' said Jenny.

But Jud, Mugsy and Blocker were ready for them, until Jud, who had other things on his mind, suddenly said, 'We'll see you around then. Maybe sooner than you think.'

With that he truculently led his troops away.

After working on him for a few days Mac eventually persuaded Rasputin to meet up with the mysterious shareholder in a desperate attempt to plead with her about the merger. But unfortunately, Ronnie had not confided her name. Stuck with a depressing stalemate, they sat in the office, wondering desperately what to do.

Outside on the pavement, Boxer was gloomily repairing a puncture in one of his tyres and when Charlotte came up he gave her a hostile look.

'Hi.'

'Hallo.' He looked away.

'What's the matter?'

'There's nothing the matter with *me*,' said Boxer childishly.

'I didn't know Jud was gonna start something, did I?'

'Course you didn't,' Boxer jeered unpleasantly.

'How could I?'

'Because,' said Boxer, getting to his feet, 'I specifically asked you if he was here to cause trouble and you said he wasn't.'

'I thought he wasn't. Honest. What do you think I am – his keeper or something?'

'Somebody should be, if it's only to lock the cage after him when he goes to bed at night.'

'Don't you talk about him like that.'

'Why not?'

'He's worth two of you any day.' They were both furious now.

'Didn't seem like that the other day.'

'You were lucky they stopped it when they did.'

'Yeah, otherwise I'd be facing a murder charge.'

'Get lost.'

She walked off angrily and Boxer was suddenly aware of Mac leaning against the wall of Outer Space.

'So there's no truth in the rumour, then?'

'Eh?'

'You're just good friends!'

'Knock it off.' Boxer went back to his puncture.

'She just came to see me and Rasputin,' said Mac.

'She did?' Boxer looked up suspiciously, the hostility growing.

'To speak up for you, that's why. To say they started it and you tried to stop it.'

'What?'

'Now, on your bike!'

But because Boxer's bike was temporarily incapacitated, he had to run after Charlotte. When he caught up with her, he could see that she had been crying. Boxer wondered if they were tears of rage or sorrow. It was impossible to tell.

'Oi.'

She walked on.

'Charlotte!'

She still walked on.

'Hang on.' He ran in front of her, panting slightly. 'I just want to tell you –'

Charlotte stopped and rounded on him. 'I don't want to talk to you.'

'At least give me a chance.'

'What for?'

'To say I'm sorry.'

Charlotte glared at him and proceeded to walk on again. Determinedly, Boxer pursued her and they talked at what was virtually a jog.

'Thanks for what you said to Mac and Rasputin about me.'

'I'm sorry I bothered.'

'Bet you're not.'

'You're *so* conceited.'

'What else do you want me to do – jump under a bus?'

'Good idea. Let's wait for one.'

'Thanks.'

'Better still, let's wait for a double-decker.'

'Where you goin'?'

'If you *must* know, to Gran's.'

'I'd better come with you.'

'Why?'

'I wouldn't want you meetin' the Big Bad Wolf.'

She slowed down to a walking pace and, as Boxer drew alongside her, she said:

'The trouble is, I've got this nasty feelin' I've probably met him already.'

'See you.'

'Is this it?'

Boxer and Charlotte were standing outside a record shop.

'Yes.'

She tried the door of the shop, but it was closed. Then she rang the bell. After a few seconds, the door was opened by a small, bright-eyed little woman in her late sixties.

'Hi, Gran.'

'Hallo, love.'

She looked quizzically at Boxer and Charlotte said, slightly grudgingly, 'Oh, this is Boxer.'

'Hallo.'

Boxer grinned. 'Hi.'

Then the local church clock struck seven and Boxer started. 'What's the time?' he gasped.

'Seven o'clock,' said Mrs Masters.

'Oh, no.' He turned and began to run as if the hounds of hell were behind him. Mrs Masters turned to her grand-daughter in surprise. 'That *was* a case of hallo and goodbye – what's happened to Jud, anyway?'

'Don't let's talk about *him*,' said Charlotte and walked hurriedly into the shop.

When Boxer arrived breathlessly back at Mac's house, Elaine said that his dad had rung ten minutes ago and told her that he was coming home from Saudi Arabia because the sheikh who employed him had run out of money and the project was cancelled.

'So both your mum and dad will be home soon. How do you feel about that, Boxer?'

'Terrific!' He was still stunned, unable to believe the news. Then the phone rang and Mac hurried to answer it. When he returned he looked cheered.

'Rasputin's found out who our mystery shareholder is.'

'Who?' asked Elaine.

'Her name's Masters – a Mrs Masters. Apparently she owns this big record shop in the middle of town.'

'Blimey,' said Boxer.

'What's up?'

'Masters – that's Charlie's name.'

'Charlie who?'

'You know, Charlotte – the girl who came to see you after the punch-up.'

'She wouldn't just happen to have a grandmother with interests in Dunmore Town, would she?'

'Dunno – but I know her gran runs a record shop.'

'It's got to be the same person, Mac,' said Elaine. 'Will you tell Rasputin?'

Mac pondered for a moment and then made a decision. 'Considering the way he's handled things so far, I'd say the answer's no.'

As Mac was shown through to Mrs Masters' living room

behind the shop by Charlotte, two familiar faces lifted their heads from the record rack. They belonged to Mugsy and Blocker.

'What's Mac Murphy doing here?' hissed Blocker.

'Dunno – but look who else is here.'

Boxer and Jenny had just arrived with a bewildered-looking Wurzel.

'I don't get this,' he was saying.

'Get what?' asked Jenny impatiently.

'What's the point of comin' in here lookin' at records when we're all stony broke?'

'We're just browsin', Wurzel,' said Boxer. 'Just browsin'.' He strolled to where Charlotte was sitting. 'Hi.'

Charlotte looked up, immediately pleased to see him.

'Hallo.'

'So that's what they call browsin',' said Wurzel sardonically.

Meanwhile, very furtively, Mugsy followed Blocker out of the shop.

'Where're we goin'?'

'To get Jud,' said Blocker, 'where else?'

In the living room behind the shop Mac was closeted with a direct Mrs Masters. Mac liked her at first sight and felt matters were getting off to a good start when she said, 'Cup of tea, Mr Murphy?' She gave him a penetrating stare and Mac found himself liking her even more.

'If it's all the same to you, Mrs Masters, I'd rather get straight down to business.'

'Good.'

'I take it I'm correct in saying you're the other major shareholder in Dunmore Town, besides Ronnie Wright?'

'I am.'

'And you know about the proposed merger?'

'I do.'

'And you're dead against it?'

'Yes.'

'Would you mind telling me why?'

'It wouldn't work.'

'Why not?'

'The fans – they're fire and water. They've been at each other's throats for years.'

'But if the merger goes ahead they'd *have* to get along.'

'Why should they?'

'If we don't merge, we'll both die. It's the only chance of survival for both clubs.'

'Dunmore Town will take its chances.'

'But what about United?'

'My dear Mr Murphy, it's not my fault that Mr Jones was rash enough to sell his ground before clinching the deal.'

'He was under the impression he had a cast-iron agreement. Mr Jones was let down.'

'Not by me.' Her voice was very firm.

'No, not by you, Mrs Masters. By Dunmore Town Football Club.'

'You mean by Mr Wright?'

'He made it clear he represented Dunmore Town in the negotiations.'

'Then he was exceeding his authority.' Her voice was even firmer.

'Not at the time he wasn't.'

'How do you mean?' There was a hint of uncertainty in her tone.

'When Wright shook hands with Mr Jones he had the full backing of the Town board, including that of your late husband. Are you telling me now that that wasn't the case, Mrs Masters?'

But Mrs Masters' directness had gone. She was at once flustered and upset. 'Please leave my husband out of this.'

'I'm afraid I can't do that.'

'Then leave – please leave.'

'Not until you've heard me out.'

'But –'

'Let me ask you a question, Mrs Masters. If your husband was alive today do you think he would renege on a deal the way you're doing?'

'My husband was dying.'

'So's my football club, Mrs Masters. Are you just going to sit there and –' But before he could say any more, Mac was interrupted by a tremendous crash from the shop and a cacophony of screaming.

'What on earth –?' asked Mrs Masters. But Mac was already on his feet and charging out of the living room. When he reached the interior of the shop he saw Boxer and Jud rolling about on the floor while display shelves and musical instruments scattered in their wake. As they fought, the other kids cheered them on.

'All right,' said Mac. 'That's it!'

Wading in, he grabbed both Boxer and Jud by the scruffs of their necks and hauled them to their feet.

'I said, *enough*.'

'Fire and water, Mr Murphy?' asked Mrs Masters from behind him.

Charlotte was putting together the last piece of a drum kit when Mrs Masters came up to her.

'How are you doing?'

'Just about finished. There's no real harm done, Gran.'

'Nice company you keep these days, Charlie.'

'They're not usually like that.'

'No?'

'Honestly – I could bash their heads together.'

'It's as I said to Mr Murphy – United and Town fans don't mix.'

'Is that why you're so dead set against the merger?'

'Yes.' Then she looked at her granddaughter in surprise. 'Why, don't you agree with me?'

'Not really, Gran.'

'But you saw what happened.'

'That was different.'

'I don't understand.'

'Well, you're right about United and Town fans. Put 'em together and you usually have a fight on your hands. But if you turn two clubs into one then you haven't got any fights, have you? I mean, they'd all be supportin' the same team, wouldn't they?'

'So, you think I'm wrong to oppose the merger?' Suddenly Mrs Masters sounded hesitant, unsure.

'I can't make up your mind for you, Gran. Hang on – there's a couple of kids who need servin'.'

As Charlotte went over to her customers, her grandmother looked at her retreating back thoughtfully.

Jason Winch was proud of himself and the way he looked – which was, to say the least, startling. He was a spectacular punk in his early teens, with a burly, dangerous-looking body, a skull tattoo on his forehead and more tattoos on his muscular arms. He looked through the window of the Masters record shop thoughtfully, watching Charlotte as she stuck up a poster.

Pressing his nose up against the glass, Jason tried to

attract her attention and succeeded. But Charlotte wasn't interested. She leant over, breathed on the plate glass and effectively misted up the area of Jason's face. He frowned and drew back.

Then Boxer arrived. As he leant his bike against the wall he became conscious of Jason's arrogant stare.

'Nice one,' said Jason.

'Eh?'

'The bike.'

'Yeah.' Boxer began to put the padlock on the front wheel.

'Wise, that.'

'Oh, yes.' Boxer's voice was cool.

'Lockin' it, like.'

'Sure.'

'You get some funny people round here.'

Boxer looked Jason straight in the eye. 'I know,' he said.

Boxer strolled nervously into the shop and immediately confronted Charlotte at the counter.

'You've got a nerve coming in here today,' she said.

'Don't be like that.'

'What do you expect?'

'Did you think I'd just stand there and let him slag me?'

'You were slaggin' him just as much.'

'He was askin' for it.'

'Of course,' she said sarcastically.

'Why do I spend my time apologizin' to you?'

'Ask yourself.'

'Gran in?'

'What do you want her for? A muggin'?'

'You don't half go on, you do.' Boxer was grinning.

'No need for you to stop and listen to it.'

'Is she, or isn't she?'

'Actually, she's right behind you.'

Boxer wheeled round like a startled cat and saw Mrs Masters sorting out a display of tapes. Full of trepidation, he went over to her.

'Mrs Masters.'

She looked up. 'Oh, it's you.'

'I just wanted to say sorry about what happened and if there's any damage, I'll pay.'

'There wasn't any, actually.'

'Oh.'

'No thanks to you.'

'I see.'

'But I think you'd better know that if anything like that happens in here again you'll no longer be welcome in this shop. Understood?' Her voice was dry and her eyes were still angry.

'Right,' said Boxer. 'There was something else, actually.'

'Really?'

'I heard what you said to Mac afterwards.'

'What was that?'

'About fans.'

'Well?'

'I just hope you won't let what happened affect whatever it is you've decided about the merger.'

'How do you know about that?'

'Mac told me I'd probably ruined his chances.'

'Did he now?'

'It wasn't what it seemed.'

'You mean that incident wasn't typical?'

'What I mean is, it wasn't about football. It was about something else, actually.'

'I shan't let it affect anything. But I have to say that what happened did confirm my worst fears about the whole idea of a merger.'

Boxer's heart sank. He really had dished it this time.

Just as he was about to argue with her again, Ronnie Wright appeared, his face wreathed in smiles.

'How are you, Mrs M.?'

'Hallo.'

Boxer's heart sank even further as he realized who he was and how Mrs Masters seemed to like him.

'Could we have a little word?'

'Of course. Come through. Keep your eye on the shop,' Mrs Masters said to Charlotte, 'especially that one over there,' indicating Jason Winch who had just come in to prop himself up on the record bar.

Boxer went up to Charlotte. 'So that's him.'

'Who?'

'The snake in the grass who betrayed us.'

'What are you on about?'

'Your beloved chairman, Ronnie Wright.'

'He's O.K.'

'So's a black widow spider until after the weddin'.'

'Look,' said Charlotte impatiently, 'he's got more brains in his head than your chairman. Least he didn't let the ground go right from under him.'

But Boxer wasn't having any of that. 'He was let down, wasn't he? Double-crossed by your chairman.'

'Who said?'

'Rasputin Jones said.'

'Well, he would, wouldn't he?'

They glared at each other and a new feeling of discord was struck between them.

★

'All this fuss about the merger,' Ronnie was saying in Mrs Masters' living room.

'I must admit it's not quite as simple as I thought it was.'

'There was always going to be a lot of aggro for you and now after what's happened, it's bound to get worse. Much worse.'

Mrs Masters sighed. 'What are you trying to do, Ronnie? Get me to think about it again?'

'Not at all. They're your shares to do with as you will.'

'But –' She was becoming increasingly worried. First Mr Murphy, then Charlotte and now Ronnie, all throwing different shades of doubt on her decision.

'All I'm doing really, Mrs Masters, is asking this question. Do you really need that amount of aggro? At your age?'

'Is there an alternative?'

Ronnie sipped his tea. 'Oh, yes, there's always an alternative.'

Boxer came out of the record shop in a furious temper over his latest quarrel with Charlotte, but his mood became a lot blacker when he found that both of his bicycle tyres had been let down. It was not difficult for him to guess who was responsible and he went banging back into the shop, looking for retribution.

Once inside, he went straight up to Jason Winch and spun him round by the shoulder. Just as he was about to hit him, Charlotte came quickly over.

'Who do you think you're shovin'?' asked Jason.

'You.'

'What's goin' on?' asked Charlotte.

'Somebody let my tyres down – and no prizes for guessing who the funny man was.'

'I didn't do it,' protested Jason vehemently.

'You were standin' there when I left it.'

'Does that prove it?'

'You didn't know it was him who did it,' intervened Charlotte.

'Of course it's him,' replied Boxer indignantly. 'I mean it's just the sort of stupid trick a punk would play.'

'What's the way he dresses got to do with it?' demanded Charlotte.

Boxer lost his temper. 'Whose side are you on, anyway?'

'Not on yours if you keep causin' bother round here.'

At that moment, Mrs Masters and Ronnie appeared from the back. Seeing the arguing trio, she said, 'I hope you're not going to start any more trouble, young man.'

Boxer glared at her, then Charlotte and then Jason.

'Forget it,' he said and slammed out of the shop.

'Blimey,' said Jenny, who had come across Boxer pumping up his tyres outside the record shop and who had listened to the whole sad story with sympathy. 'Look who's here.'

Wurzel, Pacman and Hulk, who had come up with her, stared curiously at the flash sports car parked beside the shop and the man smoking a cigar inside.

'Who is it?' asked Pacman.

'His name's Ivor Chalmers,' said Jenny. 'And he's as bent as a three-pound note. This time last year he very nearly got control of United.'

'Yeah,' said Wurzel, 'and he wasn't that particular about how he did it, either.'

'He organized a break-in at the offices and put Boxer in hospital,' continued Jenny.

'Been inside, then, has he?' asked Pacman.

'We could never prove it was him behind it,' commented Boxer ruefully.

Jenny frowned. 'But it was 'im all right, believe me!'

'Well, well. Just look at that,' whispered Boxer. 'Town's chairman himself.'

Ronnie hurried out of the shop and made his way straight to the car. Ivor pushed open the door for him and Ronnie clambered into the front passenger seat. Sliding his hands in his pockets and looking the picture of innocence, Boxer strolled along the length of the shop window as if he was casually looking inside. But in fact he was getting himself well within earshot of the conversation in the car.

'What did she say?' Ivor asked.

'She's going to ring me,' replied Ronnie.

'When?'

'Within the hour, I think.'

'And what do you reckon the reaction is going to be?'

Ronnie paused and then said very positively, 'I think all this fuss is getting through to her. I think she'll be glad to get rid.'

'You didn't tell her I was involved, did you?' asked Ivor in a voice of great concern.

'No way,' replied Ronnie.

'Very wise,' said Ivor.

Ronnie turned round in his seat and was suddenly aware of the youngsters hanging around outside.

'Shall we find somewhere a little less public?' he asked.

Rapidly, Ivor started the car and it pulled quickly away. As it did so, Boxer rejoined his friends.

'What did you hear?' asked Jenny.

'Not much,' he said glumly, 'but enough to know that

those two are up to somethin'.' He looked at the departing car thoughtfully.

When Charlotte came out of the back room of the shop, she found Jason on the wrong side of the counter, looking up at the shelves.

'Now, what do you think you're doin'?' she said briskly.

'Just 'avin' a look.'

'At what? All the records we've got are out on display.' Now she was suspicious of him, wishing Boxer was still there. She became even more suspicious when Jason grinned arrogantly at her and made his way slowly to the other side of the counter.

'Got the latest Queen album, 'ave yer?'

'Of course,' replied Charlotte briskly.

'Let's see, then,' said Jason.

'It's on the rack behind you.'

'But I want to see the disc.'

She looked at him blankly.

'I want to check the grooves, don't I? Make sure they're all right.'

'Well, of course they're all right,' said Charlotte. 'What do you think we are – a second-hand shop or somethin'?'

'Trouble is,' said Jason, 'I'm dead particular about the condition of the records I buy. Know what I mean?'

Angrily, Charlotte reached up for the disc and brought it down from its blank folder. She held it out for Jason's inspection without letting go of it herself.

'What's the matter, don't you trust me?' he asked in a mocking voice.

'You don't really want me to answer that, do you?'

'What's yer name then?'

'Why?'

'My name's Jason.'

'Oh, yeah?' said Charlotte with withering sarcasm. 'Got your Argonauts with you?'

'I'll bring them round to see you,' said Jason, not in the least abashed.

'Don't bother. Well, do you want it, or don't you?'

He grinned at her again and she reluctantly made up her mind that there was no way of insulting him.

'I'll think about it,' said Jason.

At that point Mrs Masters emerged from the back. 'Not another of your mates, I hope,' she said sharply.

'Do you mind!'

Jason, not wishing to face Charlotte's grandmother, wandered off down the shop and collided with Rasputin as he came in. At once he buttonholed him.

'You're Rasputin Jones, aren't you?' he said sneeringly.

'That's right.'

'All pensioned off now, eh? I mean the old band . . .'

'Bit before your time, eh, son?'

'I'll say,' replied Jason.

'Yeah, I can see how they would be, you still being at the nappy stage an' all.' Rasputin pushed past him and walked down the shop towards Mrs Masters, leaving Jason knowing he had received the worst of the exchange. Jason angrily banged out of the shop, almost breaking the glass in the window.

'Nice class of customer you've got,' said Rasputin.

'I think they model themselves on their favourite pop groups,' replied Mrs Masters acidly.

Rasputin grinned. 'I wouldn't know about that, of course.'

'Why should you?' she asked.

'I wonder if I could introduce myself.'

'I think I know who you are already,' she replied. '**Mr Rasputin Jones?**'

'Blimey, not another old fan!'

Mrs Masters cleared her throat. 'If you want to talk to me privately you'd better come through.'

Once in the living room she turned towards him warily.

'What can I do for you, Mr Jones?'

'I think you know. I want you to help me save your football club.'

'My football club, Mr Jones?' she replied, startled by this new approach. 'I thought it was you that was in trouble.'

'We're both in trouble, Mrs Masters. Me because I haven't got a ground and you because you're losing money hand over fist every week. Certainly a lot more than Ronnie Wright can afford to keep putting into it.'

'He seemed confident enough about the club's future when I saw him half an hour ago.'

'Whistling in the dark, my dear,' said Rasputin.

'Whistling or not,' replied Mrs Masters, 'he was certainly prepared to put his money where his mouth is.'

Rasputin began to look alarmed. 'Just what are you telling me? That Ronnie Wright is offering to buy you out? 'Cos if he is, I'll double anything he's offered you so far.'

'Oh dear, what a shame, Mr Jones.'

'What do you mean, a shame?' he asked in rising alarm.

'It's such a pity I didn't know that when I gave him my answer a few minutes ago.'

Despite Derek Cassidy's attempts to prevent them, Boxer, Wurzel, Jenny, Pacman and Hulk managed to get through to Mac. Ten minutes later Rasputin appeared and stood in surprise at his office door. 'Not you lot again?'

'Hang on a minute,' said Mac, 'they've got something to tell you that you had better hear.'

'I've got somethin' to tell you,' replied Rasputin. 'Our troubles are over.'

'What do you mean?' asked Mac.

'I went round to Mrs Masters and offered to buy her shares – but she told me she had already sold them to Mr Wright. What do you think about that?'

Mac looked aghast. 'Oh no.'

'What do you mean, oh no?' said Rasputin irritably. 'That way we get the best of both worlds, don't we? Ronnie has all the shares now, which means he's no more excuses for not going ahead with the merger and none of it cost a penny.'

Mac leaned back in his chair, conscious that he was about to give Rasputin a shock, and the kids waited apprehensively.

'So, where does Ivor Chalmers fit into all this, then?'

'Why?'

'He's only the guy who almost took over your football ground last year to turn it into a supermarket. That was before you got the same bright idea yourself and saved him the trouble.'

'All right, spare me the funnies,' said Rasputin. 'Where does Chalmers fit in now?'

'I don't know, but how come he and Ronnie Wright are blood brothers all of a sudden? And what were they doing around Mrs Masters' place about an hour ago?'

Rasputin stared at him in dismay.

Rasputin's next move was to try to get hold of Ronnie, but he was not only elusive but actually seemed to have disappeared. As Rasputin crashed the telephone back into its cradle, Mac said, 'What's up?'

'He's left the country.'

'He hadn't half an hour ago.'

Rasputin leapt to his feet.

'Where are you going?'

'To find him, where else?'

'I'll come with you,' said Mac.

'I think you'd better, just in case.'

'Just in case of what?'

'I murder him with my bare hands.'

Twenty minutes later Rasputin strode across the outer office of Dunmore Town Football Club, with Mac at his heels.

'Now, just a minute,' said Ronnie Wright's secretary, who had been doing her nails behind her desk. 'I told you Mr Wright's out of the country.'

But Rasputin and Mac totally ignored her and went straight into the boardroom, where, somewhat predictably, they came across Ronnie and Ivor drinking large scotches.

'Ronnie, you're back,' said Rasputin. 'Just a flyin' visit, was it?'

'How dare you come barging in here like that!' said Ronnie.

Rasputin took two determined steps towards him and Ronnie hastily put a table between them.

'Ronnie,' said Rasputin between gritted teeth, 'I thought we were supposed to be mates. Destined by fate to be on the same board together, right?'

'Wrong,' said Ivor Chalmers, calmly.

'And what the 'ell's it got to do with you, Chalmers?' snarled Rasputin.

'It's got everythin' to do with me, Jones, 'cos I'm the new owner of Mrs Masters' shareholding in this club.'

'She won't sell any shares to you,' said Rasputin. 'She'll only sell them to him,' and he pointed a withering finger of contempt at Ronnie.

'That's right,' said Ivor, 'and Ronnie, dear old Ronnie, will then sell them to me.'

'Since when have you been interested in football, Mr Chalmers?' asked Mac.

'Only since last year,' replied Ivor, 'since you and your companion here not only ruined a very lucrative business deal for me, but also twisted me out of a considerable sum of money.'

'Nobody twisted you,' said Rasputin. 'You just got what was comin', that's all.'

'But now,' said Ivor with great joy, 'you're gonna get what's comin' to you. Jones, you're gonna lose your club, and Murphy, you're gonna lose your job.'

Rasputin could no longer find the words and he made a grab for Ivor, snatching him by his coat.

'Fine,' said Ivor, 'do go ahead and hit me, Jones. I shan't fight back. I'll just leave it to my lawyers.'

'Don't soil your hands,' said Mac, pulling Rasputin off him.

'I'll fix you, mate,' said Rasputin, 'if it takes a thousand years.'

Charlotte was having a quiet afternoon in the record shop, with few customers, and she was sitting, reading, behind the counter when she heard the door open. She looked up to see Jason and a fellow punk of the same age come in. He had a bright mane of violently dyed yellow hair.

'Hi,' said Jason as they made their way up to the counter. 'Thought I'd drop in and introduce you to me mate. We call him "The Golden Fleece". Say hallo to the pretty lady, Fleece.'

'Hallo, pretty lady,' said Fleece, grinning at her wolf-ishly.

Then they began to saunter around the shop and finally huddled together over a rack of tapes, trying to look as if they were discussing them. They were in fact talking about the shelves directly behind Charlotte.

'That's where the best stuff is,' said Jason, 'up there on the top.'

'So what are we waiting for?' replied Fleece. 'Why don't we get it?'

'Don't be selfish, Fleece,' said Jason. 'You know the motto: share and share alike. We wait to cut in the rest of the gang, don't we?'

'So, what do we do?'

Jason lowered his voice even further. 'I've been watchin' this place for a week, right? Every mornin' about eleven the old girl trots off to the bank with the takin's, right? So, tomorrow at eleven our little lady over there will be all on her own in the shop. That is, apart from you and me and the rest of our merry men.'

They burst into spontaneous laughter and Charlotte looked towards them from her position behind the counter. What were they on about? she wondered. Suddenly she was very uneasy.

Derek Cassidy, sitting in his kiosk in Outer Space and glaring around him as usual, was surprised to find the postman delivering a letter addressed to 'Mr Cassidy – Personal'. On opening it, he was even more surprised to find that it was from Ivor Chalmers. The note was brief and to the point. He wanted to see Cassidy as soon as possible down at the offices of Dunmore Town. Slowly he reached for the telephone.

Jason and Fleece stood outside the Masters record shop, checking over their gang of three skinheads and a punk. The skinheads were Dagger, Razz and a girl called Moonie. The diminutive punk was Rose, under-nourished, street-wise, wary.

'What's the scene, Jace?' asked Moonie.

'We're goin' shoppin'.'

'What for?' asked Dagger. 'Glue?'

'No,' said Fleece, 'records.'

'What do we use for bread, man? I'm bust.'

'This is a Sally Army gig,' announced Jason grandly.

'What?' Dagger gazed at him uncomprehendingly.

'Everythin's free – you just help yourself. Know what I mean?'

The others did and started to laugh.

Mrs Masters was putting a couple of paying-in books stuffed with cheques into her bag. When she looked up Jud was staring at her sheepishly.

'Hallo,' she said.

'Mrs Masters, is Charlie in?'

Sighing, she called through to the back, 'Visitor for you, Charlotte.'

'Hi,' said Judy as Charlie emerged.

'Hallo.' She was very cool.

'I'm off, love,' said Mrs Masters. 'Back soon.'

'Look,' said Jud, wading straight in, 'it wasn't me who started that punch-up. It was 'im.'

'Funny that.'

'What do you mean?'

'That's just what he said.'

'Been hangin' around again, has he?'

'He called round to apologize to Gran.'

'Creep.'

'It's more than you did. What's creepy 'bout havin' a few manners?'

Just at that moment, Jason came roaring in with his gang, having seen Mrs Masters walking down the street to the bank. The gang scattered noisily amongst the display racks and Jud said wonderingly, 'Regulars, are they?'

'I seen 'em a couple of times before,' said Charlotte, glancing nervously round the shop. Then Jason came up looking truculent.

'Told you I would, didn't I?'

'You speakin' to me?' asked Charlotte. She was desperately worried now, sure the worst was going to happen.

'I'm not speakin' to the cat. I said I told you I would.'

'Would what?'

'Bring 'em to see you – my Argonauts.'

'Argonauts?' asked Jud aggressively.

'I'm Jason. These are my Argonauts. Good, eh?'

'Terrific. Can't think why I'm not laughin',' snapped Charlotte.

'Probably 'cos you're not supposed to,' Jason was menacing now. 'It's amazin' what trouble you can get into – laughin' in the wrong place.'

'Do you want something? Only I am busy, know what I mean?'

'I can see you are,' said Jason, flicking a sardonic glance at Jud.

'Watch it.' Jud's voice was hard.

'All right – leave it, Jud,' said Charlotte anxiously.

But Jud had no such intention. 'I'm not scared of this kind of rubbish.'

'Who are you callin' rubbish? You ain't gonna take that from him, Jace, are you?' asked Moonie.

'What do you think?' Jason tensed. 'Fancy your chances, sunshine?' he asked, squaring up to Jud.

'Any time, mate. An' if you want to find out just step outside.'

'Who needs to step outside?'

The other skinhead boys, sensing trouble, began to crowd round Jud. 'Yeah, who needs to step outside?' they chorused.

'Talk big, don't you,' said Jud, 'when there's half a dozen of you?'

'Safety in numbers.' Jason was beaming away. 'That's my motto.' He began to crowd in on Jud when Boxer and Wurzel came through the shop door. But Charlotte did not breathe a sigh of relief. She just sensed more trouble.

'This a private punch-up?' asked Boxer, summing up the all-too-obvious situation, 'or can anyone join in?'

'Just keep out of it,' sneered Jason.

'What's the matter,' chipped in Wurzel, 'don't you like it now the odds 'ave evened up a bit?'

'All right,' said Jason. 'Get 'em.'

Jud and Boxer led the others against Jason's gang. The fight quickly spread all over the shop, with display units crashing down and customers running out on to the pavement.

'Stop it,' yelled Charlotte. 'Just stop it!'

78

But Moonie started jumping up and down in front of her, imitating her voice.

'Stop it,' mimicked Moonie. 'Just stop it.'

Charlotte took one look at her, grabbed a handful of her hair and the two girls fell struggling to the ground. Fleece then began to clamber up to the shelves that held the records, pulling them out of their blank covers and throwing the discs on to the floor. Scrambling higher to get at the top shelf, Fleece suddenly felt the whole framework begin to detach itself from the wall. In awesome slow-motion, he and the shelves began to fall.

'Look out!' yelled the tiny punk, Rose, and the combatants in the immediate vicinity of the toppling edifice leapt to safety. But Charlotte was not quick enough and the shelves collapsed on top of her. The fighting stopped, the dust settled and a deep silence fell over the shop, broken only by the ragged breathing of the two gangs.

'Let's go.' Jason didn't even stop to look at the buried Charlotte and with one accord he and his gang ran out. Only little Rose stayed, transfixed by what had happened. Meanwhile Jud, Wurzel and Boxer desperately struggled to pull the shelves off Charlotte. Eventually, they succeeded and Rose helped to pull Charlotte clear.

'Gawd,' said Jud. 'She's dead.'

'No,' replied Boxer, kneeling down beside her, 'she's breathin' all right.' But despite that, she was still unconscious and there was no knowing what injury she had sustained.

'Charlie,' whispered Jud. 'Charlie.' But there was no response.

'Well, don't just stand there,' yelled Rose. 'Get an ambulance.'

Boxer darted to the telephone on the counter and began

to dial. Rose looked about her, saw that her gang had fled and cautiously began to back out of the shop. But no one stopped her. They were all too absorbed with the inert body on the floor whose breathing seemed to be becoming more shallow every minute.

The ambulance was standing outside the shop as Rasputin drove past the crowd of onlookers that had gathered, gawping at a stretcher being carried out. Slowly Rasputin pulled the wheel over and parked his Rolls a little further down the street. Then he got out and saw a police car arrive. On the stretcher he could make out a still form and beside it was Mrs Masters. She looked completely distraught.

Rasputin walked over to one of the policemen who were now standing on the pavement.

'What's been goin' on here, officer?' he asked in his grandest voice.

'Oh, the usual story,' replied the constable. 'Bunch of yobs started smashing up the shop. She got in their way,' he continued and they both looked at the stretcher being lifted into the ambulance. 'Poor kid.'

Then something caught Rasputin's eye and, as he focused, he could hardly believe what he was seeing. Jud, Boxer and Wurzel were being led out of the shop and into a police car by a couple of constables. Rasputin stared at them in mounting anxiety and then hurried down the road towards his Rolls.

'Now then.' Sergeant Grant was sitting behind a table in Dunmore Police Station while Boxer, Jud and Wurzel faced him in a grim line. 'Three visitors for you – Mr Prior, Inspector Glossop and Mr Reed.'

'Dad!' Boxer spun round to see his father's sun-tanned

face which was now sombre and bewildered. Wurzel looked up at his own dad and wished for the millionth time he wasn't in the force. It made the situation so much more complicated.

'Now, can everyone give me their attention,' said Sergeant Grant and everyone's eyes rested dutifully on him. 'Since inquiries into this incident have still not been completed, all three of you are bailed to appear again at this station tomorrow at two p.m. in the sum of twenty-five pounds. Do the parents agree to this arrangement?'

They nodded.

'In that case, I must warn you lads that if you fail to answer your bail, you will be liable to be arrested and charged separately with that offence. I must also point out to the parents that should this happen, you, in your turn, will be liable to forfeit the whole, or part of the money. Is that also agreed and understood?'

They all nodded again and Boxer's heart bled. The first time his father had been home in years and it was to see him nicked. He just couldn't bear it.

Inspector Glossop and his son, Wurzel, were driving home. Wurzel had expected a tirade, but he had not expected his father's bitter irony.

'Of course,' he said, 'when I was a young and green copper I used to have all these grand ideas. About what the future held for me.'

'Oh, yeah?'

'I used to think: I'm bright, I've got a bit of flair, I'm hard workin'.'

'Yeah, Dad.'

'There's really no reason why I shouldn't go straight to the top. Why, I even used to think I might end up as a chief constable one day or something big down in London. Glossop of the Yard. The darling of the Sunday papers and the Hammer of the Underworld.' He paused and Wurzel wondered what was coming next. 'There was just this one thing I hadn't foreseen. Just the one.'

'What's that?' asked Wurzel.

'Being lumbered with you as a son,' he said, taking a corner so tightly that Wurzel's seatbelt nearly cut him in half.

'Billy –'

'Yes, Dad?'

They were sitting in the front room with Mac and Elaine.

'Why is it that you always seem to be around when there's trouble?'

'It was four to one, Dad,' said Boxer indignantly. 'If me and Wurzel hadn't stepped in, they'd have put this kid – Jud – in hospital.'

'Somebody *is* in hospital,' Mac reminded him.

'They did that.'

'But she's there all the same.'

'How is Charlie?'

'I rang the hospital half an hour ago,' said Elaine. 'They said she was satisfactory.'

'What does that mean?' asked Boxer impatiently.

'What it says.'

'Don't they only say that when they're not so good?' Boxer persisted.

'Not necessarily.' But she spoke without conviction.

Boxer turned back to his father. 'Look, Dad, I know you've only just come home and all that, but would you mind if I went over to the hospital?'

'They aren't going to say any more to you there than they did to Mrs Masters, are they?' said Mr Reed.

'We don't know that – not till I've tried.'

His father shrugged and glanced helplessly at Mac.

'How will you get there?'

'I'll run him,' said Mac.

Boxer turned back to his father. 'Look, Dad, I'm dead sorry all this happened. On your first day back an' all.'

'Me too, Billy.'

When Boxer had gone out with Mac, Mr Reed turned to Elaine. 'That girl in hospital.'

'Yes?'

'Girlfriend, is she?'

'I think he'd like her to be,' said Elaine quietly.

'I see.' Mr Reed looked very reflective.

'Anybody sittin' here?' Boxer asked Jud warily.

'Help yourself.'

He sat down next to Jud in the hospital corridor and for a while an awkward silence reigned. Then Jud said, 'Get a bit of a roastin' from your old fella?'

'He was upset, that's all. How about you?'

'He got really nasty.'

'Sorry.'

'Thanks a lot, anyway. For steppin' in like that.'

'That's all right.'

They sat on in further silence until Jud said,

'Tough luck about your team.'

'Yeah.'

'You could always start followin' Town.'

Boxer smiled wryly.

Jud grinned. ' 'Nuff said.'

They lapsed into silence again. But it was not an un-
friendly one.

Rasputin faced Cassidy across his desk, looking at the
letter he had just been handed.

'What's this then?'

'My resignation.'

'Why?'

'As manager of this place I take it that a week's notice will
be sufficient. Murphy can always stand in. He hasn't got
much to do at the moment.'

'I see,' said Rasputin coldly, staring with hostility at
Cassidy's smirking face. 'Finally recognized your talents,
have they, Derek? Snapped you up for president of the
World Bank?'

'As a matter of fact, I'm going back into football.'

'Oh, yeah?'

'But this time on a much more satisfactory basis.'

'Where?'

'Dunmore Town.'

'You're jokin'.' Rasputin looked at him with rising fury.

'Not at all. Town have been casting envious eyes on my
work running the United Supporters' Club – work, in-
cidentally, for which I've never been paid. From now on,
Mr Chalmers wants me to do the same sort of job for
Town.'

'Does he now?'

'But on a fully professional and full-time basis.'

'Well, Derek – so he's made you an offer you couldn't
refuse?'

'That's about the size of it.'

'They're usually the first to leave the sinking ship, aren't
they?'

'Who are?'

'The rodent population.'

Cassidy's lips compressed. 'Do I take it the week's notice I've just served will start right away?'

'No.'

'I beg your pardon?'

'Do me a favour –'

'I'm afraid I –'

'In fact, do us all a favour. Clear out now.'

'I see.'

'And by the way – good riddance.'

Cassidy walked straight out and Rasputin threw a paper-weight across the room.

Boxer and Jud rose to their feet fearfully as they heard the ward door open and Mrs Masters emerged. She looked strained, exhausted – and instantly hostile when she saw the two boys.

'How is she, Mrs Masters?' asked Boxer.

'Still unconscious,' she replied shortly.

'Is she gonna be O.K.?' Jud's voice broke.

'Does it matter to you?'

'Eh?' Jud looked dumbfounded.

She turned to Boxer. 'In fact, does anything matter to boys like you?'

'Look, Mrs Masters,' said Boxer desperately, 'we –'

'No, you look. I've heard it from you before. The lot. The plain fact of the matter is that you and your cronies are nothing more than thugs.'

'But we didn't –' Jud began, but she overrode him.

'Mindless morons who start trouble just for the sake of it – who break and smash up places for the sheer joy of smashing them.'

'Mrs Masters,' began Boxer, anxious to explain, but she wouldn't let him.

'Please let me finish. I don't want to argue with you and I'm not interested in your excuses.'

'It wasn't our fault,' yelled Boxer.

'Rubbish! I've just two things to say to you and then as far as I'm concerned that's the end of the matter. Keep away from my shop in future, do you hear! And even more important, when my granddaughter recovers, keep away from her!' She paused and then said in a choking voice, 'Always assuming that she does recover.'

With tears suddenly pouring down her cheeks, Mrs Masters hurried away, leaving Jud and Boxer looking at each other in horror.

Mrs Masters came out of her living room into the shop looking tired and worried.

'Hi,' said Rasputin who was standing by the counter. She smiled wanly, not best pleased to see him.

'Sorry about your bit of bother.'

'Yes.'

'Flamin' kids.'

'Some of them, anyway.'

'How is the little girl?'

'Still in hospital, I'm afraid. As a matter of fact, I was just on my way to see her now.'

Rasputin looked at her speculatively. 'In that case, this is neither the time nor the place.'

'I suppose it's about the shares again,' she said wearily.

'I want to know one thing, Mrs Masters, and then I'll leave you in peace.'

'Well?'

'Has the sale gone through yet?'

'I haven't signed them over yet, no.' She looked at him warily.

'Good.'

'Why? It's purely a formality now, he's said he'll take them.'

'Because, Mrs Masters, I want to ask you just once more to think again and sell those shares to me.'

'Mr Jones –' she began, her voice hoarse with fatigue, 'I've aleady been through this at least twice. Once with you and once with Mr Murphy. I've promised Ronnie Wright that he can have first refusal on those shares and a promise is a promise.'

'When you gave that promise, Mrs Masters,' said Rasputin cautiously, 'you can't have been entirely aware of just what was goin' on.'

But Mrs Masters' already thin patience suddenly snapped. 'Mr Jones – please! I am at my wits' end.'

'I'm sorry. I'm only trying to tell you that –'

'I've just lost my husband, my granddaughter is in hospital, and here you are, badgering me about a few wretched shares in what's really a very unimportant little football club. You've already said this is neither the time nor the place, so if you'll excuse me I'd like to lock up and go to the hospital.'

Pointedly she went to the door and opened it.

'Right,' said Rasputin glumly. He wanted time, but it was running out. Then he had a brainwave.

'Like a lift to the hospital?'

'I've my own car, thanks.'

'Right,' said Rasputin again, making his way out. She locked the door quickly behind him.

'Hi, Gran.'

'Charlotte!'

She was conscious and, although very weak, she managed a smile for her gran.

'How are you feeling, love?'

'Bit soggy between the ears – still, nothin' new about that.'

The sister came up and grinned at them both.

'How is she?' asked Mrs Masters.

'A very lucky young lady. Shaken up, but apart from that, she'll live.'

'I'm so glad.' Mrs Masters began to cry and Charlotte protested.

'Gran, don't start.'

'What do you expect?' she said as she fumbled in her bag for a hanky without success. 'I've been worried to death about you.'

'Here, use mine.' Charlotte passed her the hanky and her grandmother blew her nose loudly.

'Well,' said Charlotte, 'what's been happenin'?'

Pacman, Hulk, Jenny and Mugsy were sitting on the steps of the police station, gloomily waiting for news. All feared the worst. The doors opened behind them and Boxer, Wurzel and Jud emerged. They all looked rather mystified.

'What's goin' on?' asked Jenny.

'Dunno.'

'What do you mean?' demanded Pacman.

'They're droppin' the charges,' said Boxer in a bewildered voice.

'Why?' Mugsy was amazed.

'That's the bit we don't know,' replied Wurzel.

Inspector Glossop, Mr Prior and Mr Reed then came out of the station.

'What's goin' on, Dad?' asked Wurzel.

Inspector Glossop glared at him. 'Well, what it amounts to is that they're not proceeding any further with the matter. At least – not as far as you lot are concerned,' he said grudgingly.

There were whoops of delight from everyone except Boxer, who still looked extremely puzzled.

'But why?'

'Well, son,' said Mr Reed, 'apparently they got a telephone call this morning from the girl's grandmother up at the hospital.'

'So?'

'The girl regained consciousness –'

'Great,' said Boxer and Jud in unison. Then they stared at each other self-consciously.

'And cleared you lot completely.'

'In fact,' said Mr Prior in a surprised voice, 'according to the sergeant in there, if you hadn't had a go the way you did, it could have been much worse.'

Wurzel looked up at his dad reproachfully. 'Yeah, well I did tell you, Dad, didn't I? Can't understand why you didn't believe me.'

Inspector Glossop gave his son a strange look as if he wanted to belt him, but couldn't. Then he said in a strained voice, 'Can I offer anyone a lift into town?'

'You could drop us off at Outer Space, Dad.'

'You weren't included in the invitation, son.'

'Thanks, Dad.'

Inspector Glossop took the adults off in his car, leaving the kids on their own. Boxer turned to Jud.

'Do you reckon she'll be back yet?' asked Boxer.

'Who?' Jenny's face was blank.

'Mrs Masters – from the hospital.'

'There's only one way to find out,' said Jud. 'There's a bus now. Let's get on it.' And they raced towards the stop.

Rose stood uneasily in the record shop, waiting for Mrs Masters to finish serving a couple of customers. Then, when the door opened, she hid behind a record display, for she had caught a glimpse of Jud and Boxer coming in. Mrs Masters looked up with a smile of welcome.

'Boxer – Jud. Hallo.'

'We just wanted to say thanks,' said Jud. 'For what you told the police.'

'It was the least I could do,' she smiled, 'after what Charlie told me.'

'How is she?'

'Why don't you go and find out?'

'You mean she's back?'

Boxer and Jud hurried through to the back room while Rose continued to lurk.

Meanwhile, in the boardroom of Dunmore Town Football Club, Ivor was beginning to give Ronnie Wright a bad time.

'I must confess, I'm rather baffled, Ronnie,' he said with a cold smile.

'Why's that, Ivor?'

'I can't understand the delay in getting those shares transferred.'

Ronnie shrugged. 'You must have heard about the trouble she's had. I just didn't want to bother her.'

'You'd be doing her a favour – giving her one less worry.'

'What's the hurry? She's given me her word. There's nothing to worry about, Ivor.'

'Oh, I'm not worried, Ronnie.'

'Then –'

'You're the one who should be worried.'

'Why's that?'

'Well, if anything goes wrong, you're the one who's going to miss out on a fat little profit – not to mention finding a bankrupt football club on your hands.' As he spoke, Ivor was still smiling.

'I'll get on to her first thing in the morning.'

Ivor laughed without humour. It was not a pleasant sound. 'Never put off till tomorrow the things you can do today.'

'But –'

'Go over to the filing cabinet and get out a stock transfer form and get her signature. Now.'

'She may not be in.'

Ivor picked up the telephone. 'This is a wonderful invention.'

Grudgingly, Ronnie began to dial.

Mrs Masters put down the telephone and looked at Rose, who was hovering uncomfortably in the shop.

She hesitated and then said, 'I was wonderin' how she was – that girl who got 'urt yesterday.'

'She's home now. No real harm done.'

'Good.'

'Are you a friend of Charlotte's?'

'No, nothin' like that. Just wondered how she was, that's all.'

'Do you want to come and say hallo? She's here.'

Rose instantly looked alarmed. 'No, thanks. Gotta be goin'. See you.' And with that she scampered out.

Mrs Masters was pouring tea for them all and at the same

time wondering why Charlotte, Boxer and Jud were looking so sombre. She hoped they hadn't been quarrelling
again.

'What did he want, Gran?' asked Charlotte.

'Mr Wright? Oh – he just wanted to pop around and clear
up a bit of business.'

'It wouldn't be about Grand-dad's shares, would it?'

'That's right.'

'Did he say anything about a Mr Ivor Chalmers?'

'Who on earth's he?'

'He's never mentioned him to you?'

'I don't think so. Why? Should he have done?'

'I just thought he might have,' said Charlotte thoughtfully. 'Specially if what Boxer here's told me happens to be
the truth.'

Mrs Masters looked at Boxer's worried face quizzically.
'I think you'd better tell me all about it,' she said.

Half an hour later an ingratiating Ronnie Wright arrived
in the shop and Mrs Masters led him through to the living
room. But directly he saw Charlotte, Boxer and Jud, he
began looking uneasy. Detecting this, Mrs Masters said,

'Don't worry about these two. They've just called in to
see Charlotte.'

'Oh, I see.' He seemed relieved. 'How are you, Charlotte?'

'I'm all right, thanks.'

'Good.'

He produced the form from his inside pocket. 'If you'd
just sign here, Mrs Masters,' he said, laying it on the table.

Boxer could see his hand trembling slightly.

'Where I've put the pencil mark.' Ronnie was clearly
anxious to get the signing over and he smiled encouragingly

at her as she studied the form. Then he started as she said, 'There must be some mistake.'

'Mistake?' Boxer could see Ronnie Wright was instantly tense.

'According to this, I'm assigning the shares to you.'

'That's right.'

'I'm sorry, but wouldn't it be much simpler to assign them straight to him?'

'Him?' Ronnie Wright stared at her, sweat breaking out on his forehead.

'Mr Ivor Chalmers. I mean, that's who they're really going to eventually, isn't it?'

'I don't know who you're talking about,' he said, going crimson.

'The name doesn't mean anything to you?'

'Chalmers?' began Ronnie. 'Chalmers? I can't say it –'

'He runs a chain of supermarkets,' said Boxer.

'Does he?'

'And a big flash car.'

'Really?'

'The one you were sittin' in with him yesterday,' continued Boxer. 'Right outside this shop.'

'What nonsense!'

'I've got plenty of people who saw you. Witnesses, like.'

Ronnie paused, the sweat still gathering on his forehead. 'Look, just what's goin' on here?'

'That's just what I'd like to know,' said Mrs Masters. 'Now are you going to sign that form?'

'No, Mr Wright. I don't believe I am. Not now.'

'But you gave me your word you'd sell those shares to me.' His voice rose on a high panicky note.

'And I'm still prepared to do that providing I can have

your word that the minute I do, you won't resell them to Ivor Chalmers.'

'You can't impose conditions like that,' blustered Ronnie. 'When those shares are in my name, I can sell them to who I like.'

'True – and as long as they're in *my* name, I can sell them to who I like. And after what I've heard I certainly won't be selling them to you.'

'You've been got at, haven't you?'

'*Got* at?'

'By that failed pop-singer, Rasputin Jones.'

'Mr Jones has also made me an offer for them. Yes.'

'As I thought.'

'In fact the more I think about the idea, the more I like it. And by the way, I don't see him as a failure. I have every record he ever made.'

'Look,' Ronnie's voice took on a wheedling tone, 'this is Ronnie Wright you're speaking to – you can trust me, you know that.'

'So, you'll give me your word, then?'

Nonplussed, Ronnie just stood there. Then he spat out, 'You're a very difficult old lady.' And he stalked furiously from the room.

Once he had gone, the three kids treated Mrs Masters to a well-deserved, spontaneous burst of applause.

Having alerted the rest of the gang, Boxer and Jud hurried across to Rasputin's office, where he and Mac were miserably looking into a bleak and hopeless future.

'Not you lot,' said Rasputin as they trooped in. 'I can't stand it. I mean, they used to 'ave things like you back in the old days of Greece. The gods used to send 'em down

94

to torment blokes who'd committed some unspeakable crime against humanity.'

'Harpies,' said the Hulk, trying to be helpful.

'That's it, Harpies,' said Rasputin. 'But I've not committed any unspeakable crimes against humanity, have I?'

'Oh, I dunno,' said Mac. 'There's always that last record.'

'Very funny,' said Rasputin. 'Anyway, I told you before, you lot are banned from this place.'

'We've got something to tell you,' said Jenny.

'Yeah,' said the Hulk, 'wait till you hear what we've got to tell you, Rasp.'

Rasputin looked at him in disbelief. '"Rasp"!' he said. 'My God, now I've heard the lot. Out!'

'We've got a message for you from Mrs Masters,' said Boxer.

'Oh?'

'Yeah,' said a grinning Wurzel. 'Something about the shares she's sellin'.'

'What about them?' asked Mac.

'Well,' said Wurzel, 'the way I heard it – and this lot will correct me if I'm wrong – if you still want 'em, you can have 'em.'

'What are you on about?' said Mac impatiently. 'Those shares are already promised to Ronnie Wright.'

'Yeah – well, they've just been unpromised,' said Jud.

'Since when?' asked Rasputin in rising excitement.

'Since Mrs Masters found out who the shares were really promised to.'

'This wouldn't be your idea of a sick joke, would it?' asked Rasputin menacingly.

'Course not,' said Jenny.

'Well – what do you think?' Rasputin asked Mac.

'I should get on the blower.'

'To hell with the phone,' said Rasputin, grabbing his coat and diving for the door. 'If this is a joke, I'll kill you, every one of you – with my bare hands.'

When Ivor Chalmers heard the bad news from Ronnie, he thumped the boardroom table so hard that he hurt his hand. Nursing it, he yelled at Ronnie, 'You idiot!'

'I told you what happened . . .'

'If you'd clinched the deal right away nothing would have happened. The shares would have been in your name and there wouldn't have been a blind thing the silly old bat could do about it.'

'I must say, I do feel a certain responsibility for what happened.'

'Oh, you do, do you? That's nice to know.' Ivor Chalmers' cold smile was so fixed on his features that it might have been carved from granite.

'So, I'll tell you what,' continued Ronnie, 'if you're still keen to join the board I can always sell you some of my shares.'

Chalmers almost had apoplexy. 'Listen, I don't want to *join* the flamin' board: I want to *be* the board. Otherwise I just don't want to know. Get me?'

He got up and, for a moment, Ronnie thought he was going to physically attack him. Then he slammed out only to find Rasputin in the outer office.

'Ivor!' said Rasputin. 'Takin' our bat home, are we?'

'I'll fix you, Jones – if it's the last thing I do – I'll really fix you,' he snarled.

'What, *again*?' asked Rasputin innocently.

Ivor Chalmers walked swiftly away and Rasputin leapt

to the door just as the elusive Ronnie Wright was going to shut it in his face.

'Now, be friendly, Ronnie,' said Rasputin, closing the boardroom door.

'Board members only in here – it says so on the door.'

'How true, Ron. Still, I'm sure an exception can be made in my case, can't it? Seein' I do now happen to be the majority shareholder in this football club.'

'What are you on about?'

'I'm on about fifty-five per cent. That's the extent of my shareholdin' in this place – or certainly will be, anyway, when Mrs Masters' shares come through and I've put them alongside the ones I've been quietly moppin' up over the last few weeks. So, Ronnie, why don't you tell me all about your troubles, eh?'

'What troubles?' he said bleakly.

'Your financial troubles, you know, all the outstanding debts you can't meet any more now that slimy Ivor's slipped off. Then, when we've talked about all that, we'll talk about another thing.'

'Which is?'

'How soon we can convene a special meetin' to get the new chairman sworn in.'

'But I'm the chairman,' Ronnie protested vehemently.

'You were,' said Rasputin.

While Rasputin and Ronnie were having their high-powered if hardly friendly meeting, the kids were having another one – and this was definitely much more friendly. Sitting in Charlotte's living room, Boxer kicked off the discussion.

'Now the clubs are mergin' what we have to decide is just where we fit in.'

'How do you mean?' asked Mugsy.

'Well, for starters there's the Junior Supporters' Club.'

'But we've already got a Supporters' Club at Town.'

'Yeah, but that's run by adults, isn't it?' said Boxer.

'By adults for adults,' put in Wurzel. 'All they're into is playin' snooker, aren't they? I'm tellin' you they won't want to know about our age group, mate.'

'What we want,' said Jenny, 'is the sort of set-up we used to have at United – with our own committee and everythin'.'

'Right,' said Boxer.

'We've already got the gear,' enthused Wurzel. 'It's really just a matter of findin' a room to put it all in.'

'Where would we find that?' asked Mugsy.

'Down at the ground,' said Jenny.

But Pacman was doubtful. 'But will they let us have anythin' down there?'

'Well,' said Boxer, 'we won't know till we ask.'

Mac was leaning moodily against one of the machines in Outer Space, reading a newspaper, when Boxer approached him.

'Do me a favour, Mac?'

'What now?'

'We want to re-form the Junior Supporters' Club.'

'You do, do you?'

'What do you reckon?'

Mac put down his paper and treated Boxer to a long stare. Then he said, 'I think it's a good idea.'

'Great!' Boxer was overjoyed.

'Anything that keeps you lot off the streets *must* be a good idea.'

'So we can go ahead?'

'I can't say that.'

'Why not? You're the manager, aren't you?'

'Who said?'

Boxer was completely nonplussed. 'You're not leavin', Mac?'

'I'm bound to be.'

'But *why*?'

'For the simple reason that I earn my living managing football teams. In case you hadn't noticed, Town already has a manager in the shape of Mr Sydney Gregg.'

'He's rubbish, isn't he?'

Instantly, Boxer realized he had said the wrong thing, for Mac looked angry.

'Is that his fault?'

'What do you mean, Mac?'

'Look, Syd Gregg's only a football manager, he's not Brian Clough, Bob Paisley and Superman Three all rolled into one.'

'So?'

'So he can't make a Kenny Dalglish out of a pig's ear. All he can do is his best with players he's stuck with, and if the players are rubbish then his best isn't going to be good enough, is it?'

'He's still not in your class as a manager, Mac.'

'That's not the point, old son.' Mac was calming down now and Boxer felt relieved. Yet he also knew, instinctively, how desperately worried Mac was.

'Course it is,' Boxer insisted. 'When you were pickin' the United team you always said it was the best players who got picked. I mean you couldn't afford to be sentimental about it. So, if it applies to players it has to apply to managers. Right?'

'Wrong,' said Mac. 'Gregg's fifty-two years old, maybe more.'

'What's his age got to do with it?'

'It's got this to do with it.' Mac was getting angry again. 'If I'm out of work, I've got every confidence I won't be out of work for long. But at his age, if Gregg finds himself out of work, he's finished.'

'Mac –'

'No. If somebody else wants to put him out into the street and on to the dole queue they can get on with it. But don't ask me to do it, that's all.'

Mac folded up his newspaper carefully and walked out of the amusement hall. Boxer watched him go in dismay.

'Now then, what the 'ell do you want?' Rasputin confronted Wurzel and Jenny outside the squash courts. He had just played rather a good game, narrowly beaten his opponent and was feeling that all was right with the world. The merger, his squash, his feeling of well-being, had put him in a buoyant mood, so he looked at the two kids with just a little less cynicism than usual.

'We just wondered if you'd heard yet – that's all,' said Wurzel.

'Heard what?'

'About Mac.'

'What about Mac?' asked Rasputin blandly.

'You mean you haven't heard?' said Wurzel incredulously.

'Now look here, sunshine, don't start playin' games with me.'

Then Wurzel began to tell him and Rasputin's good mood very quickly began to evaporate.

★

Boxer, now back living with his parents, was at Mac's house rooting out the last remnants of his scattered possessions, when Rasputin arrived looking furious. Boxer quickly scooted upstairs, while Mac showed Rasputin into his sitting room.

'You must be psychic,' Mac said.

'Really?'

'I've been trying to get hold of you all morning.'

'Well – you needn't have bothered.'

'Oh?'

'I heard about it from a couple of scruffy kids down at the squash club! They seemed to know more about your plans than I do – as usual.'

'I already told you – I've been trying to get hold of you all day.'

'Don't you think,' said Rasputin, fuming, 'that I should have been the first to be told about it? I mean – I only pay the wages round here.'

'All right,' said Mac, flaring up. 'Boxer came to see me yesterday about something else – and it just slipped out. I s'pose he must have passed it on.'

'You bet he did. Just give it to me straight. True or false?'

'True.'

'Just like that.'

'No, not just like that.'

'When did it happen then?'

'When did what happen?'

'When did you get this bang on the 'ead that brought on the brainstorm?'

As they spoke Boxer and Elaine were coming down the stairs and they both stopped to listen to the rising tempers in the sitting room.

'Town have already got a manager,' Mac was saying.

'Syd Gregg?'

'Yeah.'

'I'll tell you what, Syd Gregg isn't fit to lace your boots. You know it and I know it.'

'He's still the manager down there.'

'*Was* the manager.'

'What do you mean?'

'One of the first things I'm doing is chuckin' 'im.'

'Oh, yes?'

'Now, you listen to me, mate. You've told me more than once, it's your job as manager to pick the team, right?'

'Right.'

'Now, I'm telling you, it's my job as chairman to pick the picker. And if I decide Syd Gregg isn't picking any teams of mine, then that's the way it's gonna be.'

'Your decision, Mr Chairman,' said Mac quietly.

'Good.'

'And it's my decision as to whether I'm prepared to step into his boots.'

'You're contracted to manage my football club,' said Rasputin firmly.

'Wrong, Mr Chairman. I'm contracted to manage Dunmore United Football Club – a club which, like Dunmore Town, no longer exists. So don't talk to me about contracts, Mr Chairman. Because your contract isn't worth the paper it's written on.'

'You know what I think?' Rasputin said with sudden venom.

'What?'

'I think this whole thing stinks.'

'What do you mean by that?' asked Mac ominously.

'You've been got at.'

'Got at?' Mac sounded amazed.

'By some other club,' rasped Rasputin, 'and you're using this Gregg business to get out of your contract.'

Mac glared at Rasputin and tried to control himself.

'Know what your problem is, Mr Chairman?'

'My problem is puttin' faith in you.'

'No, your problem is that you judge everybody by your own low – non-existent – moral standards. Now, before you say anything else you might regret, why don't you just leave?'

'I'll leave when I've had my say.'

'You won't. You'll leave now.'

Elaine, still standing on the stairs with Boxer, knew all too well that note of finality in Mac's voice. With great speed she hurried into the sitting room, only to find Mac and Rasputin in eyeball to eyeball confrontation. Rasputin then turned, saw her, and stalked out, brushing past Boxer. A few seconds later they heard the front door slam so hard that Boxer thought it would come off its hinges.

'What on earth's goin' on, Mac?' asked Elaine.

Mac turned to Boxer. 'Will you tell her, or shall I?'

'Me?' Boxer looked very worried.

'Yesterday,' said Mac, ignoring him, 'I made the mistake of telling this young man, here, that I had no intention of taking on Syd Gregg's job. So he tells his mates and they take it upon themselves to pass the information on to our chairman. Before I'd even had a chance to tell him myself.'

With that, Mac abruptly left the room and, once again, the front door slammed loudly.

'I only told Wurzel 'cos I was so worried,' said Boxer miserably.

'Don't worry,' said Elaine.

'But I do – and what about Mac?'

'Oh, he's just mad about the way things have happened. It was pretty stupid of Wurzel to blurt it all out.'

'Yeah,' said Boxer. 'I think I'll go and tell him.'

For the third time, the front door took a pounding.

'Talk of the devil.'

Boxer saw Wurzel emerging from the Outer Space office.

'Yeah, I'm back on the staff.'

But Boxer was not interested in Wurzel's re-employment.

'You are a nit,' he pronounced. 'A big, steaming nit.'

'What are you on about now?'

'It was you who told Rasputin about Mac.'

'What was it – a state secret or something? All I was tryin' to do was to get Rasputin to get Mac to change his mind. See what I mean?'

'Well, you didn't. In fact you made things a thousand times worse.'

'Oh, no.' Wurzel was genuinely contrite.

'Rasputin and Mac have just had a flamin' row and now it looks like there's no chance of 'im stayin' on.' Boxer was furious and Wurzel's miserable expression said everything about his feelings.

Then Charlotte, Jud and Mugsy arrived and Boxer told them about Wurzel's big mistake. Then Jud, much to Wurzel's relief, changed the subject.

'We was thinkin' of goin' over to the ground to see if there's anythin' we can do about this room for the Junior Supporters' Club. Charlie knows the club secretary.'

'Oh, yeah?' said Boxer apathetically.

'You comin'?'

'Dunno. It won't be the same if Mac's not runnin' things any more.'

In the end Boxer decided to go with them, but the penitent Wurzel remained at Outer Space, trying to show enthusiasm at the return of his old job. Sweeping grimly at the generous tide of sweet papers, he suddenly recognized Rose.

'I know you, don't I?'

'You talkin' to me?' she said defensively.

'I'm not talkin' to the machines,' said Wurzel. 'Weren't you with that mob of skinheads who started the punch-up in the record shop?'

'No.'

'You were. I saw you.'

'I wasn't *with* them. I just 'appened to be in there, didn't I?'

'You sure?' asked Wurzel suspiciously.

'Course I'm sure. Anyway, what's it to you?'

'We just don't want any trouble-makers in here, that's all.'

'You in charge round 'ere?'

'Yeah.'

'Well, what did you think I was gonna do? Start chuckin' space invaders through the plate-glass windows?'

Wurzel took a look at her tiny size and said, 'You watch it, that's all. 'Cos I'm watchin' you.'

'Don't worry, I won't wreck your place.'

Wurzel wandered off and Rose glared after him.

'Adolf Junior!' she said as she resumed playing with a handful of coins.

When Rasputin strolled out of the tunnel he could see that Syd Gregg was acting as a referee to a training game between the first and second teams. The players were wearing a variety of different strips and the play was rough.

Ostensibly Syd Gregg seemed jovial enough, but Rasputin could sense an edge to the man that smacked of resentment – particularly when he saw who was bearing down on him. The same could be said of Ronnie Wright, who was watching from the touch-line. In his eyes Rasputin could see the pain of a man who still thought his club had been hijacked.

But any amount of bad feeling was not going to put Rasputin off. He had arrived, buoyed up with a new idea that Wurzel, of all people, had confided in him. It was an interesting idea, possibly a very clever idea. Wurzel's voice still resounded in his ears: 'Some of the best British teams ever 'ave 'ad two men in charge: Cloughie and Taylor, Mercer and Allison. Know what I mean?' Rasputin did, and he reckoned he was in with a chance. He had already been to see Elaine and obtained her willing cooperation. Now he was here to take the plan further, if he could.

'Mornin',' he said cheerfully to Ronnie.

'Hi,' Ronnie returned with a perfunctory smile. 'How does it feel to be chairman?'

'No worse than it felt bein' chairman of United. Good of you to say you'd stay on at the meetin' last night. As vice-chairman, of course.'

'Not at all,' said Ronnie, inwardly writhing.

Then they turned their attention to the game, only to see a young reserve forward come dribbling through and Knocker Clarke, one of Town's more rugged players, going in for a savage tackle that brought him down. Gregg blew his whistle immediately.

'Come on, boss,' said Knocker, 'I was only goin' for the ball.'

'Yes, and if you'd gone any higher you'd have taken his head off. This is supposed to be a practice game, Knocker – not the sixth round of the Cup. Cool it!'

Knocker offered a helping hand to the young player, but it was angrily pushed away.

'Temper, temper,' said Knocker.

On the touch-line, Ronnie Wright shook his head and laughed. 'He only knows one way to play, does Knocker,' he said.

'Yeah,' replied Rasputin. 'Dirty.'

'What a character, though.'

'Laugh a minute. Bet he doesn't think so, though.' Rasputin nodded towards the hobbling young reserve.

'Knocker's a fine defender though – and captain,' insisted Ronnie. 'He's also been a loyal servant of the club over the years.'

'If you say so, Ronnie.' For all his deviousness, Rasputin didn't like dirty play.

Gregg blew his whistle to end the game and the players trooped off to get their ball. Ronnie, accompanied by Rasputin, then strolled over to Gregg.

'Lads are in good shape, Sydney,' said Ronnie.

'I reckon they're just about ready.'

'Let me introduce you to our new chairman, Rasputin Jones – Sydney Gregg.'

They shook hands uneasily.

'For a moment,' said Rasputin, 'I thought you were goin' for *The Guinness Book of Records*.'

'How come?'

'For the first time in the history of football someone gets sent off in the practice game.'

'Knocker Clarke, you mean?' said Gregg, laughing. 'Always a bit of a boisterous character.'

'So was Godzilla,' said Rasputin and they both laughed, sensing each other's hostility.

'You're finished for the mornin'?' asked Rasputin.

'Yeah.'

'I'd like a word with him in private, if you don't mind, Ronnie?'

'Be my guest.'

Rasputin led Gregg away, knowing how very much Ronnie *did* mind.

Mac opened his front door to find Syd Gregg on the doorstep. He looked at him in surprise. As rival managers they had been friendly but not on socializing terms.

'Can I come in?' he asked.

'Sure.'

Mac led him through to the sitting room.

'Cup of tea?'

'No thanks – I've got to get back soon.'

'Look,' said Mac, trying to come straight to the point, 'if it's your job you're worried about, forget it. I've already made it clear to Rasputin Jones that I'm not after it.'

'I'm sorry to hear that.'

'What?'

'Jones wants you for his manager – not me.'

'But he can't have me.'

'Yeah – but that doesn't help me at all.'

'Why not?'

'Because he's not wearin' me as manager – either way.'

'Has he actually said that?' Mac's voice took on an angry edge.

'Look, Mac, I don't have to go to the North Pole to know it's flamin' cold there.'

'Fair enough, but I still can't see why you're sorry that I won't take the job.'

'I'll tell you why. Because if you're in, I'm not necessarily out.'

'Explain.' Mac was looking at him with increasing curiosity.

'Well, if you're prepared to take on the job as manager then he's prepared to keep me on as deputy.'

'Has he told you that?'

'Yes.'

'And why would he do that?'

'That way, he gets the manager he wants and a nice easy conscience. Also, it keeps him cosy with the old Town fans, doesn't it? Show 'em all that this is a genuine merger and not just a take-over by United.'

'I see what you mean,' said Mac slowly. 'But what about you? How do you feel?'

Gregg gave him a big warm smile. 'Look, Mac, I'm fifty-two years old and a realist. Now, where would I get another job in football management? Besides, there is the other factor.'

'And what's that?'

'I'm a fan of yours. Always have been.'

Later, Mac talked over the situation with Elaine.

'What are you going to do?'

'If Rasputin goes along with the idea,' said Mac slowly, 'how could I refuse?'

'But there's something bothering you still, isn't there?'

Mac grinned a little ashamedly. 'There *is* something.'

'What's that?'

'Would I have agreed to being deputy if the position had been reversed?'

'Well?'

'I don't think so.'

'But then you're not fifty-two.'

'There is that.' Mac looked at her thoughtfully.

Knocker Clarke was giving Gregg a lift back from Mac's house.

'I still don't believe you're gonna do it,' said Knocker incredulously.

'Why not?'

'I'd have thought you'd have too much pride, boss.'

'When you get to my age, Knocker, pride's something of a luxury. Besides, soccer's a funny game, full of ups and downs.'

'What's that supposed to mean?'

'Mac Murphy's top of the heap right now, but who knows what might start goin' wrong for him in a few months' time.'

Knocker began to laugh. 'Why – you crafty old devil!'

'How many times have I told you, Knocker,' said Gregg gently, 'when you 'aven't got it in the legs any more you've got to use what you've got up here.' He tapped his forehead and Knocker laughed again. It was not a pleasant sound.

Meanwhile the kids had not been idle. They already had permission from Beryl, Dunmore Town's typist, to use an old storeroom as the headquarters of the Junior Supporters' Club, and even Boxer cheered up a little as they planned to decorate it. But their plans were to be quickly frustrated by the arrival of Derek Cassidy. The gang were packing rubbish into paper bags when he stormed in, looking furious.

'And what do you think you lot are doin'?'

'We were just wonderin' when you were going to raise your head, Mr Cassidy,' said Boxer gloomily.

'Well, these are our new premises,' said Jenny innocently. 'Least they will be when we've tarted the place up a bit.'

'New premises?' asked Cassidy, acidly.

'Yeah,' said Charlotte. 'For the Junior Supporters' Club.'

'Is this supposed to be some kind of joke?' The smile slowly left Cassidy's face.

'No joke, mate,' said Jud. 'We got permission from Beryl in the office.'

'Oh, you did, did you?'

'She didn't think anyone would object.' Charlotte's voice was firm.

'But I object.'

'Why?' asked Jud aggressively.

'I'll tell you why. In the first place if you wanted a room you should have come to see me. I am, after all, general manager round here. Not Beryl. And in the second place, even if you had, your journey would have been quite unnecessary anyway since the very last thing I'm prepared to put up with here is your wretched Junior Supporters' Club. I've had too much trouble with it in the past.' Cassidy ended on a triumphant note.

Revenge, thought Boxer, that's what he's taking, and enjoying every minute of it.

'You can't stop us,' said Wurzel, blunt as usual. 'You never could before.'

'But that's where you're wrong, see,' said Cassidy with delight. 'I've already stopped you by rendering you absolutely unnecessary.' He grinned at Wurzel with almost manic pleasure.

'What do you mean?' asked Boxer. 'Every club needs junior supporters.'

'But this place already *has* a Junior Supporters' Club.'

'What?'

'In fact it was one of the very first things I introduced here. A Junior Section of the Senior Supporters' Club.'

'That's not the same,' said Jenny.

'No, it isn't.'

'Then –'

'It's better organized, better run and certainly a lot less trouble. Oh, and just one other thing. All applications for membership go through me, so if any of you feel like joining, do let me know, won't you?'

Cassidy gave them all the nasty look which exactly spelt out their chance of joining. Then he stared at their equipment and said joyfully, 'And if you don't get rid of all this junk – and yourselves – in half an hour, I'll call the police.'

Although infuriated by Cassidy's attitude, Boxer was considerably cheered when he heard about Mac's decision to become manager of the merged clubs. Meanwhile, Rose was still trying her luck at Outer Space when Charlotte arrived to sit alone at a table. After cautiously watching her for a while, Rose approached her, apprehensively clutching a cup of coffee.

'O.K. if I sit here?'

'It's a free country.'

Rose sat down hesitantly.

'They've been talkin' about me, 'aven't they?'

'Have they?' asked Charlotte coolly.

'Tellin' you I was one of the gang what busted up your gran's shop.'

'Are you saying you weren't?'

'I was there when it 'appened, yeah.'

'But not with them?' Charlotte was sarcastic now.

'Sort of. What I mean is – well, they were the only other

kids I know and I didn't know they went in for that kind of thing. Anyway, since then I've had nothin' more to do with 'em. Honest.'

Charlotte looked at her but said nothing.

'You don't believe that, do you?'

'I s'pose I do,' said Charlotte slowly. 'I've certainly never seen you with any of 'em. So, who are your mates now then?'

'Haven't got any, have I? Least, not since I stopped runnin' about with that lot.' She glanced at Charlotte anxiously. 'Bet you got lots of mates, though, ain't yer?'

'No more than anybody else, I s'pose.'

'You're in this club thing, aren't you?'

'Which club thing?'

'Junior Supporters' Club. All the kids in 'ere 'ave been talkin' about it.'

'Sort of.'

'Can anyone join?'

'Course. But chance would be a fine thing.'

'How do you mean?'

'Well, the way things are goin' now it doesn't look as if there's even going to *be* a Junior Supporters' Club.'

Mac, irritated by Knocker's dirty play during morning practice, decided the time had come to assert his authority and set the kind of standards he felt the game should uphold. So, without waiting for Knocker to change, he called him into his office. He arrived sweating and slightly apprehensive, covering up his unease with an aggressive truculence.

'You wanted a word, boss?'

'Yes. I'll come straight to the point. I think it's only fair to tell you personally that I don't see you goin' on as captain with the new team.'

Knocker gave him a sour look. 'You mean the new skipper's Bobby Brent – formerly skipper of Dunmore United, right?'

'Right. Bobby gets the job for only one reason – because I happen to think he's the best man for the job.'

'You're the boss.'

'And another thing – if I see you play dirty again you'll lose your place.'

'Oh, come on.'

'If you want to play for me, you play my way. The right way.'

Knocker shrugged. 'Can I go now, boss?'

'Why don't you do that?'

Knocker turned away abruptly, opened the door and passed Rasputin coming in.

'Hallo, Knocker,' he said, but Knocker said nothing and brushed past him.

'Been upsettin' him, 'ave you?'

'Not half as much as I will do if he doesn't stop playing football like he was King Kong.'

Rasputin grinned at him affectionately. 'Great to be back in harness, eh?'

'By the way, the kids want a Junior Supporters' Club here.'

'Well, I hope you sent 'em off with a flea in their ear.'

'No need,' said Mac craftily, 'Derek Cassidy did it for me.'

Rasputin's eyes narrowed. '*The* Derek Cassidy? I'll get rid of him.'

'Is that a good idea?'

'Best I've had today.'

'You can't go round sacking people without good reason. Not nowadays.'

'I've got a good reason. Every time I look at him I feel ill.'

'Try telling a court that and they'll skin you alive.'

'What court?' asked Rasputin indignantly.

'The court he'll take you to for unfair dismissal. And if those are the only grounds you can come up with, then he's going to take you to the cleaners, isn't he?'

Rasputin stared at him angrily. 'So, we're stuck with him?'

'I didn't say that.'

'Then what *did* you say?'

'Supposin' Derek took it into his head that he didn't really want to work for you any more?'

They eyed each other speculatively, then Rasputin said, 'And why should he suddenly do that?'

'Well,' said Mac, 'they do arise. Differences of opinion, you know. Like the Junior Supporters' Club.'

'But I don't want the flamin' Junior Supporters' Club,' snapped Rasputin.

'Are you sure about that?' asked Mac blandly.

'What it all boils down to is this, Derek.' Cassidy was facing Rasputin across the desk. 'Mac wants the kids in and you want the kids out. Right?'

'Right.'

'And that's what I call a radical difference of opinion – that I, as chairman, have to rule on.'

'But it's none of Mac Murphy's business,' protested Cassidy.

'It's none of his business at all, really.'

'Ah.'

'If we're going to play it by the book.'

'Which we should.'

'So, if I decide after all to come down on his side, then you, in your new position as social manager, would be understandably furious.'

'Correct.'

'No more than I would be, Derek, if I'd been put in that position. In fact, if it was me, I'm afraid I couldn't let me get away with it.'

'You couldn't?'

'Good Lord, no.'

'I see.' Cassidy looked at Rasputin pensively.

'You see, Derek,' said Rasputin confidingly, 'I'd have to put it on the line. I'd have to say that either I am the social manager round here or I'm not. And if we're goin' to have this malarkey every time the fancy takes you, well, you know what you can do with your job.'

'You would, would you?' Light was beginning to dawn in Cassidy's self-protecting mind.

'Of course I would, Derek. Because, let's face it, I'd have been put in a position where resignation would have been the only course left open to me, wouldn't I?'

'I suppose so,' said Cassidy. 'On the other hand, of course, all this is purely hypothetical.'

'How do you mean, Derek?' asked Rasputin, the triumph dying in his voice.

'Well – it's presupposing that, preposterous though the idea might be, you would in fact come down on Mac Murphy's side in the dispute.'

'Yeah, I know. I suppose it does, doesn't it, Derek?'

Cassidy gazed at Rasputin, suddenly seeing the trap door yawning at him.

'Don't tell me he didn't resign,' said Mac when he saw Rasputin a few minutes later.

'He didn't,' said Rasputin doggedly.

'You did tell him you were vetoing his decision about the kids, didn't you?'

'I told him.'

'He was supposed to resign on principle.'

'Yeah. Well, nobody told that to Derek, did they? Besides, he don't have any principles. He's just got this built-in survival kit.'

'Oh well,' said Mac, 'it's an ill wind.'

'What's that supposed to mean?'

'At least the kids will be happy.'

Rasputin looked at him very shrewdly. 'That wouldn't, by any chance, be the main object of the exercise as far as you're concerned?'

'You know, Mr Chairman,' said Mac, 'I sometimes think you think I'm a lot smarter than I really am.'

'I'm goin' to watch you, mate.' Rasputin grinned wolfishly.

'Do that,' said Mac.

Charlotte left her bag on the table when she went from the Outer Space coffee bar to the loo. When she got back, she saw Rose and said, 'You comin' over to the Junior Supporters' club?'

'I thought you'd got slung out?' said Rose in surprise.

'So we've just been slung in again.'

'Blimey.'

'So, why don't you come?'

'Not tonight.' Rose suddenly seemed very agitated.

'Look, it'll be all right,' said Charlotte compassionately.

'No – I –'

'I'll be with you.'

'The – the thing is, I promised Mum I'd be home early. Help her with the cleanin' and all that.'

'Are you sure? I mean, you're not just sayin' that?'

'Course not. I'll see you tomorrow.'

'O.K. Wish you'd change your mind, though.'

'I told you,' said Rose almost sharply, 'I promised me mum.'

'See you then.'

Charlotte picked up her bag and hurried out. Rose sat down at the table and stared into nothing.

In the storeroom the kids were sitting around the pool table, having a meeting about decorating the place and raising the money to do so. Then Wurzel came rushing in, looking worried.

'You lot seen the notice stuck up outside the club office?'

They hurried over to the office and stood grimly looking up at the proposition Cassidy had penned:

DUNMORE F. C. SUPPORTERS' CLUB
JOIN THE NEW JUNIOR SECTION OF THE DUNMORE
F. C. SUPPORTERS' CLUB – DUNMORE'S ONLY
OFFICIAL SUPPORTERS' CLUB.
APPLICATION FORMS CAN BE OBTAINED FROM THE
CLUB OFFICE. ALL YOUNGSTERS WELCOME.
MEMBERSHIP FOR YOUR FIRST TWELVE MONTHS
IS – FREE!

The gang looked at the notice with despair.

'That's bribery,' said the Hulk.

'They're gonna kill us off before we've even started.'

'That's right,' said Charlotte. 'I mean, who's gonna cough up subs to join us when they can join them for nowt?'

Boxer, however, had an idea. 'Listen, what have they got that we haven't?'

'Lots, knowin' Cassidy,' said Wurzel dispiritedly.

'But what have they got that we don't want?' insisted Boxer.

'What?' Jud sounded completely mystified.

'Cassidy. That's what they've got. I mean – who'd want to join a club with him in charge?'

'But they won't know that when they join,' said Jenny.

'And when they do – just how long do you think they'll stay? And that's where we come in.'

'So the sooner we get the place tarted up, the better,' said Wurzel with returning enthusiasm.

'Let's all empty our pockets and see how much we've got for paint between us,' suggested Pacman.

The gang all thought this was a good idea, although Mugsy looked a bit rueful as he thought of all the proceeds from his rackets being handed over. But then he remembered he wasn't operating so many since he had got mixed up with Boxer and Co. Suddenly Charlotte, who was going through her handbag, exclaimed:

'I've been robbed!'

'Are you sure?' asked Boxer while the others gaped at her in surprise.

'I'm positive. When I was over in the Outer Space coffee bar I definitely had a fiver. Now it's gone.'

'Who was around?' asked Boxer, watching the others.

Charlotte thought for a moment. Of course, she said to herself, Rose was around.

When Charlotte confided her loss to the rest of the gang, most of them also reckoned that Rose had taken the money, thus confirming Charlotte's worst suspicions. But they were so totally hostile to Rose that Charlotte, to her own surprise, found herself defending her, eventually stalking off angrily in face of the doubts of the gang.

Troubled by Charlotte's attitude, Wurzel and Boxer decided to investigate and they hurried to Outer Space to see if Rose, who they knew was obsessed with the machines, was flush – which at least would provide some circumstantial evidence. But when they bumped into her she was simply hanging around, staring at the machines moodily. She soon detected their hostility.

'Charlie not with you?' she asked.

'She's gone home,' said Wurzel aggressively, 'very upset. Somebody nicked her spendin' money right out of her bag.'

'That's terrible.'

'You wouldn't by any chance know anythin' about it, would you?' pursued Wurzel.

'Me?'

'Well, you were with 'er this afternoon which is when it happened. I just wondered if you'd noticed anything, that's all.'

'Like what, for instance?' she asked suspiciously.

'Like anyone messin' with her bag?'

'Afraid I didn't.'

'Pity,' said Wurzel as he strode off to work, ''specially for Charlie.' He left Rose standing there, all too conscious that she was his number one suspect.

Despite everything, Charlotte invited Rose to help her sell programmes at the match that afternoon. Charlotte was still very suspicious, but part of this suspicion was eased when her grandmother said that Rose had visited Charlotte in hospital, deeply concerned about her. Charlotte felt very confused; she liked Rose, felt sorry for her, even felt protective about her. Yet, there was definitely something about her that was not right, that didn't hang together.

Charlotte was standing by one of the turnstiles under a banner advertising DUNMORE JUNIOR SUPPORTERS' CLUB, when Rose came running up.

'How you doing?'

'All right.' She handed Rose a sheaf of membership application forms and then burst into raucous voice. 'Join the Junior Supporters' Club! Get your application forms here!'

But the crowd hurried past, apparently uninterested.

'I'm sorry someone nicked your money,' said Rose.

'Who told you?'

'Wurzel. It's dead rotten is that.'

'That's the way it goes.'

'Do you want a coffee?'

'No, thanks.'

'I'll pay,' said Rose eagerly.

Charlotte laughed. 'I can afford a coffee. Anyway, we get a free one in the club after the game. Thanks anyway, though.'

Rose smiled shyly. ''S all right.'

The crowds pressing around the turnstiles were thicker now and among them were Jason and Fleece, jostling through in their usual aggressive manner. Then Jason suddenly grabbed Fleece by the arm.

''Old on. Do you see what I see?'

'Blimey, it's little Rose.'

They could see her standing by Charlotte, giving a membership form to a youngster in Dunmore colours.

'Well, well,' said Jason. 'That girl she's with – isn't she

the one that got clobbered in the ding-dong down at the record shop?'

'It is. Now what the 'ell's Rose doin' hangin' around with 'er?'

Jason looked thoughtful for a moment. Then he said, 'Tell you what – why don't we ask her?'

Fleece looked at him and grinned. 'Yeah, why not?'

They ambled over to her and Jason said:

'Hi.'

'Hallo,' she replied sullenly.

'Where've you been?'

'Busy.'

'Giveaways, are they?' Jason asked, holding out his hand for the form. Reluctantly she gave him one. He read it and turned to Fleece.

'Why don't we join then?'

'I wouldn't bother if I were you,' said Charlotte, recognizing them all too well. She moved over to join Rose.

'Why not?' asked Fleece indignantly.

''Cos you'd be wasting your time. You'd never get in.' Charlotte was clearly unafraid of them and Rose, who was terrified, looked at her with admiration.

'Toffee-nosed lot, aren't they?' Jason remarked unpleasantly, 'your Junior Supporters' Club?'

'It's not that,' said Charlotte.

'Then what?'

'It's just that we draw the line at lettin' scruff in. Know what I mean?'

Rose felt a freezing sensation draw over her as Jason gave Charlotte a wide, dangerous, humourless grin.

'Anyone tell you you've got a big mouth?' he asked.

But Charlotte remained calm. 'Why don't you buzz off?

Or shall I call a couple of those coppers over and say it was you who smashed up my gran's shop last week?'

'You've got a *very* big mouth,' Jason said, but he moved off with a sneer, Fleece moving somewhat hurriedly in his wake.

'You want to watch them two,' whispered Rose. 'They're dangerous.'

'So's crossin' the road,' said Charlotte, waving a membership form in another kid's face.

The visitors were 2–0 at half-time and Rasputin and Mac had begun to realize that some of the Town players were much weaker than United's had been. As for the gang, the results were extremely depressing but not half as depressing as Derek Cassidy's P.A. announcement at half-time:

'*I want to draw your attention, ladies and gentlemen, to something that will be of great interest to all young Dunmore fans – the new Junior Section of the Supporters' Club.*'

'Oh, no,' said Charlotte. 'This is it.'

'*Yes,*' continued Cassidy, '*this season the Dunmore Supporters' Club will be opening its doors to all youngsters interested in joining. This means not only special cut rates for trips to all away games, but ready access on certain nights of the week to all the club's other facilities. And remember – junior membership of the Supporters' Club is free, yes, quite free, for the first twelve months.*'

The gang had gathered together to listen to this dismal announcement, and the news was brought home with even greater force when a young boy sporting Dunmore colours came up to them with a form.

'Oi!'

'Yeah?' asked Jud.

'This form I got. It says it's gonna cost me two quid.'

'That's right.'

'Well, accordin' to what that bloke just said membership's free.'

'His club's different,' said Charlotte.

'What's different?' the boy asked suspiciously.

Wurzel came in with a quick, but ineffective bit of sales talk. 'Well for starters, there's a difference in quality, isn't there? I mean, if he *has* to give his away, well, that gives you an idea of what a right load of rubbish it is, doesn't it?'

'I dunno,' said the boy. 'But I can join 'em for nuffin' and that's what counts.'

As he abruptly walked away, he screwed up the membership form Charlotte had given him and chucked it on the ground.

Mac gave his players a pep talk at half-time, saving his real anger for a private word with Knocker.

'That soft second goal they got.'

'Yeah?'

'That one was down to you, son.'

'Oh, come on, boss,' protested Knocker. 'They split us wide open.'

'Yes,' said Mac slowly, 'that's because you went for the man instead of the ball.'

'Look –'

'As a result of which he made a right mug of you. You're paid to be a sweeper with this team, sunshine, not a hitman. Now, let me tell you, any more of that stuff and you're off the park and turnin' out with the stiffs next Saturday. Do you get me?'

For a moment Knocker looked at Mac as if he could kill

him. 'I get you,' he snarled as he slammed out of the changing room.

Mac's criticism gave Knocker the necessary motivation, even if he was in the foulest mood possible. Early on in the second half he pounced on a loose ball, controlled it with expertise, sprinted with it for a few yards and scored Dunmore's first goal. The kids went wild with delight on the terraces and the players rushed into a self-congratulatory huddle until Knocker broke in on them, hissing, 'Break it up – let's get another one.'

As the players raced down the field, only two youngsters in the ground were not caught up in the action. Predictably, they were Jason and Fleece who were making their way down a flight of steps that led to a storeroom behind the Senior Supporters' Club bar. They watched a bar steward emerge through an open door, carrying a box. Behind him Jason and Fleece could see crates of beer and boxes of cigarettes. As the steward put his box down and carefully locked the door, they could hear the whine of a burglar alarm in the background. When he had disappeared, Jason turned to Fleece and said:

'Think how much booze there must be in there – and fags! Must be worth thousands.'

'You know what that whinin' noise was, don't you?'

'Alarm.'

'Right.'

'So, now we know, don't we?' grinned Jason. 'They got an alarm.'

They began to move surreptitiously around, grinning at the thought of the challenge that had just been presented to them, to say nothing of the loot.

*

Meanwhile there was a tense silence on the pitch as a Dunmore corner was taken. Then a group of players rose for the wall, but it was Knocker who climbed the highest, hammering the ball down with his head and sending the goal-keeper sprawling hopelessly. Once again the kids went crazy with delight, while Rasputin, in the directors' box, and Mac, in the dug-out, got to their feet and yelled.

But Knocker's determination was not over yet as he turned to the players thronging around him, fiercely shouting:

'Another one – we've got to get another one.'

The players streamed back for the kick-off and Boxer squeezed Charlotte's arm till it hurt. 'We're gonna do it,' he whispered through clenched teeth. 'We're gonna do it.'

But all this excitement did not penetrate the minds of Jason and Fleece as they stood calculatingly on the terraces among the crowds.

'You're not thinkin' of havin' a go at that place, are you?' said Fleece.

'No?' replied Jason with a confidence that Fleece couldn't understand.

'But what about the alarm?'

'Bit of a problem, that,' he grinned.

'Are you sayin' you've got a way round it?'

'If there was no way of getting round burglar alarms, there'd be no such thing as burglary, would there?'

He grinned again as Knocker dispossessed an attacking player of the ball, straightened it up and headed off up-field as the kids screamed themselves hoarse. He put through a beautiful long ball, one of the Dunmore strikers collected it on the edge of the box, turned to shoot, but was flattened by a defender. The referee whistled frantically, pointing to the penalty spot, and Boxer hugged Jenny with delight.

Knocker then placed the ball on the penalty spot, stepped back, came in as if he was going for a whack, but instead rolled the ball gently into the goalmouth as the goalie dived the wrong way.

The crowd erupted, the kids danced together on the terraces, the referee blew the whistle for full-time and Knocker leapt in the air, squarely punching a fist at the sky. Then he was mobbed by his team-mates.

There was quite a celebration going on in the changing room when Mac and Gregg strolled in, with Knocker balancing a full pint of bitter on his head. But the look on Mac's face killed the hilarity stone dead. In the ensuing silence, he said:

'Just a few wee words before we all get carried away and kid ourselves that we've won a famous victory.' The silence deepened. 'The fact is, we didn't. We got away with it – just.' The silence became stunned. 'Now get this, all of you, and get it good. What I expect from professional footballers is a full ninety minutes of effort right from the kick-off and nowhere else. Not a frantic forty-five when you find yourselves in the sort of trouble you should never have been in in the first place. Get me? So if you lot are thinking of spending the rest of the season playing for me, don't give me another first-half performance like that ever again.'

He went quickly out and when he had gone, Knocker turned to the other players. 'Yeah, thanks, boss.' All the elation had gone and he was furious. 'I'll remember that next time we're in dead trouble – when somethin's needed above and beyond the call of duty. I'll remember it and he can flamin' well forget it.'

*

Despite the jubilation, the gang were still depressed at the way Cassidy had upstaged them. Then Boxer remembered they had a hundred quid in the bank from the old Junior Supporters' Club and he reckoned it was fair enough to use it for their new set-up. This would at least pay for the decorating of the old storeroom, not that that would make any difference to the present situation. Amidst groans from the others, Wurzel agreed to decorate in futuristic style. But as he was going through the door, he suddenly stopped dramatically and searched his pockets while the others stared at him in consternation.

'What's up?' asked Charlotte, while Rose watched her strangely.

'That's funny. I could have sworn when I came in here I'd got nearly a quid's worth of silver in my pocket. Now wait a minute, let me think. Oh yeah, when I came in from the game I walked over there –' He began to walk over towards the sink. 'And I put the money down right here.' He turned back to the rest of the gang in high drama. 'And now it's gone. Somebody took it.'

There was consternation all round until Rose said quietly, 'I took it.'

They turned to stare at her, realizing with a sense of shock that she was holding the silver in her hand.

'It was a set-up, wasn't it, Wurzel?' she said.

He shrugged, suddenly uneasy.

'You left it to see if I'd take it, to prove I took Charlotte's money – to prove I went through her bag. Right, Wurzel?'

Wurzel nodded, unable to deny what he had done.

'So you can keep your money,' said Rose, thrusting it into his hand. 'And what's more, you can keep your rotten club.'

She then ran out of the room with Charlotte after her.

'Rose, hang on a minute. I want to talk to you.'

But Charlotte, was too slow and as she emerged from the club, she was just in time to see Rose running through the gates.

Charlotte yelled, 'Rose, wait.' For a moment she considered giving chase, but she knew she would never out-run her. Turning back to the club, she saw Wurzel standing by the door.

'Now look what you've done,' she snapped.

'I was only tryin' to help.'

'Who do you think you are, Sherlock Holmes?'

'But –'

'Got a few tips off your dad, did you?'

'He did give me the odd one, yeah.' Wurzel looked worried and upset, as if he couldn't understand why Charlotte was so angry.

'Well, you've blown it now,' she said, 'you really have.'

While the kids began to decorate the storeroom, Charlotte spent most of her time worrying about Rose. Eventually she managed to track her down in the street.

At first Rose did not want to see her, but Charlotte was so forceful that finally Rose agreed to take her back to her council flat. Rose made some coffee and they both went through to the living room. There was a photograph of a woman and a man on their wedding day placed on the cluttered sideboard and while Rose went over to a cheap record player and started to sort through the records, Charlotte picked it up.

'This your mum and dad?'

'Yeah,' said Rose hesitantly.

'They out for the night then?'

'Mum works till nine o'clock most nights and, of course, Dad's away.'

'Oh.'

'Yes,' said Rose sharply, 'workin' abroad.'

'Like Boxer's dad?' asked Charlotte.

'How do you mean?'

Somehow Charlotte felt that Rose was now very much on her guard.

'Well, he was on a job for nearly eighteen months,' said Charlotte, 'over in the Middle East.'

'That's where my dad's workin',' said Rose.

'Really? Small world. Bet you don't half miss 'im though.'

'Yeah,' said Rose distantly, 'I miss him all right.'

'Still,' said Charlotte in a conciliatory voice, 'they get good money on those jobs in the Middle East.'

'Terrific,' said Rose.

'And your mum works a leisure shift, does she?'

'Sort of,' said Rose simply. 'She has a job on the pumps down at the petrol station.'

'Does she like it?' Charlotte asked.

'She hates it,' replied Rose, 'only we need the money, don't we?'

'S'pose you do,' said Charlotte, giving Rose a strange look and wondering why they needed the money if her father was earning such a terrific salary.

Rose suddenly realized her mistake. 'What I mean is, we can't get any of Dad's money till he's finished, see. That's the way they work it. So, while he's away we just have to manage the best we can, know what I mean?'

'Not easy,' said Charlotte thoughtfully.

'No,' said Rose.

She quickly put a record on and turned the machine up

as loud as she could. Charlotte listened, still wondering about Rose.

While Charlotte was talking to Rose, the gang was having a desperate meeting about how they could provide competition to Cassidy's 'official' Junior Supporters' Club. Finally, Pacman came up with a brilliant idea.

'Why don't we run a talent contest? We could build up to a final.'

There was considerable support for the idea and Boxer said, 'We could build an entire disco round it and fill in with records – at least until we get the thing going properly.'

'We've still got a problem though,' said Jud.

'What's that?' said Boxer.

'If you want to run a contest you need to have a prize.'

His comment threw an instant damper on the general enthusiasm, but Boxer supported him.

'Jud's right, but what sort of prize could we possibly offer that would pull anybody in?'

'We couldn't,' said Wurzel. 'But that still doesn't mean we can't have it.'

There was a surprised reaction to this rather extraordinary remark, but Wurzel continued, 'Hear me out. What I'm sayin' is that there's no way we could come up with a prize that was big enough, right?'

'Right.'

'But that doesn't mean,' said Wurzel, 'that there isn't somebody else who could.'

'Like who?' asked Jud.

'Ask me no questions,' replied Wurzel blandly, 'and you'll be told no lies. Just leave it to your Uncle Wurzel, right?'

*

Rasputin was busy writing cheques in his office when there was a knock at the door.

'Yeah?'

Wurzel came in, wearing an overall. 'Mr Jones . . .' He spoke in an ingratiating manner that was quite sickly to hear.

'Well?'

'It's – it's about something we have in common.'

'*We* have something in common?' Rasputin looked at him with a combination of suspicion and amazement.

'Clubs,' said Wurzel.

'As in Indian?'

'You will have your little joke,' Wurzel chortled, having a good creep. 'I believe – rumour has it – you're opening a new disco-club down at the ground.'

'Correct.'

'And we are in the process of opening a new Junior Supporters' Club down there.'

'So?'

'I'm sure you want to get your project off the ground with a bit of a bang.'

'So?' Rasputin asked, getting visibly more irritated.

'So, maybe we should get together,' said Wurzel with a sycophantic grin. 'Scratch each other's back, know what I mean?'

Rasputin practically gibbered in a cross between rage and astonishment, 'Is this a dare?'

'Who dares wins,' replied Wurzel coolly.

'Come in,' said Charlotte as Rose hesitated at the door of Outer Space.

'I can't.'

'You've got to.'

'I just *can't*.'

'You've got to face them someday.'

'But not now.'

'Rose –'

'Yeah?'

'Remember what we said?' Charlotte took her arm and led her gently but firmly into the amusement hall.

'Now let's get this straight,' said Rasputin gently. 'You're runnin' a talent contest to boost your club for which you want me to offer a prize. Because by doing that it's gonna boost my club. Right?'

'Right.'

'Now,' said Rasputin with equal gentleness.

'Yes, Mr Jones?' asked Wurzel eagerly.

'Get out.'

'Hear me out first,' Wurzel pleaded. 'We're not askin' for a money prize.'

'That's wise of you, my son.'

'All we want from you is a spot.'

'A spot?' Rasputin looked mystified.

'On the bill at your club. The first prize for the winner of our contest is a guaranteed spot at your new disco one night.'

'What's in it for me?'

'Publicity.'

'What kind?'

'Think of the headlines, Mr Jones, think of the national headlines. Rasputin Jones, that zonkin' great star of yesterday is lookin' for a zonkin' great star of tomorrow. And, while he's at it, yet again helpin' the poor deprived youth of the area.'

Rasputin gazed at him, his eyes beginning to shine.

'What do you think?' asked Wurzel.

'I'll tell you.'

'Yeah?' Wurzel looked apprehensive.

'I think it's a flippin' good idea.'

Charlotte and Rose were finishing a game on one of the Outer Space machines when Jason and Fleece came across, looking menacing.

'Everybody 'appy?' he asked.

'Can't happen often,' said Charlotte. 'Not with you two around.'

He gave her one of his threatening smiles and stepped towards her, while Rose cowered back. 'It's your mouth again,' he said.

'Hi.'

Jason and Fleece wheeled round to see Boxer, Jud, Pacman, Hulk and Mugsy standing there.

'Just leavin', were we, lads?'

'You gonna make us?' asked Fleece.

'We'd enjoy that,' said Jud.

'Talk big, don't you, when it's five to two.'

Mugsy, Hulk and Pacman moved off, leaving Boxer and Jud.

'Now then,' said Boxer, 'what were you sayin'?'

Jason and Fleece sneered, backed off and slowly walked away.

'My heroes!' said Charlotte, batting her eyelids at them.

'Well,' said Boxer, doing his John Wayne bit, 'a man's gotta do what a man's gotta do.'

Just then, Wurzel emerged from Rasputin's office looking stunned. He came up to the others as if he was walking in a dream.

'What's up?' said Boxer.

'It's Rasputin.'

'Tell you to get out, did he?'

'No.'

'Then?'

'He's in,' said Wurzel. 'You've no idea how far he's in!'

'How far?'

'Two hundred smackers plus a guaranteed booking.'

'Blimey,' said Boxer.

'That's what *I* thought,' gasped Wurzel.

Cassidy was furious about Rasputin's decision to back the kids' idea, but Rasputin, anxious to feather his own nest with the right kind of publicity, told him that the idea was going ahead and that the weaker of the two Junior Supporters' Clubs would go to the wall.

'We'll have to see,' he told him. 'May the better outfit win.'

But Wurzel was not so pleased when Jason and Fleece turned up in the club to fill in a talent contest form.

'There must be some mistake,' said Wurzel. 'We're lookin' for groups – not 'ead-bangers.'

'You refuse to let us enter?' asked Jason aggressively.

'You catch on quick.'

'Why?'

'I could think of half a dozen reasons,' said Wurzel. 'But here's one to be goin' on with.'

'What's that?'

'I don't like your face or his.'

'Frightened we might win?'

'No,' said Wurzel. 'I'm frightened of catchin' somethin'.'

For a moment it looked as if Fleece was going to take a swing at him, but Jason put a hand on his arm.

'Hold it,' he said and led him away.

Wurzel watched their departure in surprise.

Wurzel would have been even more surprised if he had seen them walking into Cassidy's office, outside which a large notice read:

DUNMORE SUPPORTERS' CLUB.
JOIN THE JUNIOR SUPPORTERS' SECTION NOW.
GET YOUR MEMBERSHIP FORMS HERE.

Jason, grinning at the dumbfounded Fleece, knocked on the door.

'Enter.'

Jason and Fleece did as they were bid.

'Can I help you?'

'Excuse me,' said Jason politely, 'is this where you come to join the Junior Section?'

Cassidy put on his most winning smirk. 'It is.'

He went over to a filing cabinet and dug out a couple of forms, while Jason winked at the still puzzled Fleece behind his back.

As Cassidy handed him the form, he said, 'Thank you, sir. How much is that, please?'

'Oh, membership is absolutely free for the first season.'

'Fantastic. Thank you so much, sir.' Jason was all innocent charm and Fleece gazed bemusedly at this sudden new character.

Meanwhile, well pleased, Cassidy beamed at them.

'Just one thing, sir.'

'Yes?'

'The talent contest.'

Cassidy frowned slightly. 'What about it?'

'They say if we join up with you lot we can't enter.'

'Who's they?'

'The kids runnin' it over in the clubroom.'

'They said that, did they?'

'Yeah.'

'Just one moment.'

Cassidy stalked angrily out, leaving Fleece to say, 'Look, I don't want –'

'Listen,' said Jason, 'why don't you just trust me?'

Cassidy furiously told Rasputin all about it. Finally, an exasperated Rasputin said, 'All right, you've made your point.'

'Well?'

'Yes, you're quite right, that talent contest must be open to everyone.'

'And that includes members of my Junior Section?'

'Correct.'

'So will you point that out to them, Mr Chairman, or shall I?'

'Why don't you tell 'em, Derek?'

'I'm not sure that –'

'I mean, think of all the pleasure it would give you.'

Cassidy met Rasputin's eyes and, not liking what he saw there, said, 'Certainly,' and hurried out of the room.

A few minutes later, having been told by a triumphant Cassidy that they were eligible, Jason and Fleece left the office.

'I still don't get it,' said Fleece.

'Get what?'

'Why're you so bothered about gettin' us into that contest? I mean, all right, with your brother on lead guitar we can just about make a noise. But there's no way we're gonna win it.'

'So who's bothered about winnin'?' asked Jason.

'Then what are we in for?'

'Money,' said Jason with deadly simplicity.

'What money? You don't mean the two hundred quid? We don't stand a chance, I've told you that.'

Jason laughed in a sinister, indulgent way. 'Not the two hundred quid.'

'Then what?'

'A lot more than that, mate. A lot more.'

'I don't get you.'

'You will,' said Jason, still laughing.

When Jason, his elder brother Eric, and Fleece turned up for the audition, Wurzel and the gang were hopeful that they were going to be rubbish. But they weren't. They were good and this was so surprising that everyone was horrified, for there was no way they could stop them taking part in the competition.

But if the gang was down in the dumps, so was Bobby Brent, United's original captain, who had wandered into the changing room to hear Knocker lecturing on future main tactics to half a dozen members of the first team squad, who were cooling off after a day's training.

After the meeting Bobby had a few forceful words with Knocker.

'Just how long have you been coach round here?'

'Talkin' a bit of tactics, that's all,' said Knocker carelessly.

'Funny, they didn't sound much like Mac Murphy's tactics.'

'That's true,' he replied with a grin.

'So?'

'I don't know what you're on about.'

'What I'm on about is this, Knocker,' said Bobby firmly. 'As long as Mac Murphy's coach of this side and I'm captain of it – we play it his way. Not yours. Understand?'

Knocker sneered unpleasantly. 'Yes, captain. Three bags full, captain.'

'Oh, and just one more thing.'

'Yeah?'

'No more tactical discussions behind Mac's back, eh?'

'Such touchin' loyalty in one so young.' But now Knocker's sardonic mood had changed and he was glaring at Bobby.

'You want to try it,' said Bobby. 'Break the habit of a lifetime.'

'Anything else, skipper?'

'Let's hope not.'

Angrily Knocker walked out, brushing past Mac at the doorway.

'I heard some of that,' said Mac when Knocker was safely out of earshot.

'Nothing I can't handle, boss.'

'Sure?'

'Yeah, I'm sure.'

Bobby picked up his bag and hurried out of the changing room while Mac stood there, a thoughtful look on his face.

Jason, Eric and Fleece lounged up against the wall, watching a couple of draymen delivering crates of beer to the bar steward outside the club storeroom.

'There's the burglar alarm console,' said Eric, 'down by the side door.'

Then Cassidy came bustling round the corner. 'Hallo,' he said, looking at them quizzically.

'Mr Cassidy,' said Jason, with hurried presence of mind. 'Just the man we're lookin' for.'

'Oh, yes?'

'This is my big brother, Eric,' continued Jason. 'He's dead keen to join the Junior Supporters. The only thing is, he's a bit worried in case he's too old.'

'How old are you, Eric?' asked Cassidy pleasantly.

'Nineteen.'

'I would have thought the Senior Supporters' Club would be more your cup of tea.'

'Whatever you say, Mr Cassidy,' said Eric respectfully. 'You're the one who fixed it up for us to enter the talent contest then? Jason has been tellin' me –'

'That's right.' Cassidy looked pleased.

'Dead good of you to go to all that trouble just for our sake.'

'Not just for your sake,' said Cassidy gently. 'There was a principle at stake. Everything all right, is it?'

'Fine,' said Jason. ''Cept for the judgin', of course.'

'The judging?'

'You know, the actual heats, like. It seems that's goin' to be done by the kids themselves. Now, far be it from me to say that they'd be bent about it, but they've made it pretty clear what they think of our chances. Particularly as they're what you might call the rival Junior Supporters' Club round 'ere.'

'They actually said that?' asked Cassidy, immediately outraged.

'They'd deny it, of course. But that's what they said.'

'Very well,' said Cassidy striding away angrily. 'I'll sort that out.'

When Cassidy had disappeared Eric said, 'You know somethin', little brother?'

'What?'

'When you first told me about that bloke Cassidy I thought you were exaggerating.'

'Yeah?'

'But you weren't, were you? I mean, he's every bit as stupid as you said he was.'

Naturally enough, Cassidy went straight to Rasputin and eventually a weary Rasputin had to agree that he had a point and that bona fide judges were important. Meanwhile, Eric, Jason and Fleece maintained their surveillance on the bar stores, noticing with delight that the steward had left the key to the alarm in the lock.

'Did you see what I saw?' hissed Eric.

'Yeah,' replied Jason. 'He left the key to the alarm in the lock.'

'I'm not with all this,' whispered Fleece gloomily.

'How do you mean?' Eric sounded impatient.

'Well – even if he has left the key in there – the alarm's still on, right?'

'Right.'

'So how are we goin' to get in there without setting it off, like?'

'A good point that, Fleecy. And definitely one we're goin' to have to take into consideration.'

'You got a plan then?' asked Jason quietly.

'What do you think?' said Eric, yawning widely.

The gang were furious when they found out that they were not going to be allowed to act as judges, particularly as they were told by Cassidy who delighted in passing on the news. He told them the judges had to be impartial and that there had already been complaints about the lack of this. Knowing who was doing the complaining, Wurzel tried to point out how much trouble Jason and Co. would make – but his advice fell on deaf ears. So, while the gang tried to find some 'impartial' judges, Eric was explaining to Jason and Fleece in the Outer Space coffee bar how he would deal with the padlocks on the storeroom door.

'No problem to a decent pair of wire-cutters,' he said in a low voice.

'The burglar alarm?' whispered Fleece desperately.

'That,' said Eric, 'is where my master plan comes in nicely. We're gonna have to plant someone in that store-room to switch it off.'

While Eric was putting his plan into operation, Mac had decided to drop Knocker for one game to make sure he realized who was boss. This was greeted with rage by Knocker, who, thinking Bobby Brent had split on him, tried to pick a fight which Mac separated just before it came to blows.

Half an hour later the kids approached the still ruffled Bobby and asked him to be a judge, an offer which he accepted with pleasure, for he liked the gang and always reckoned he knew quite a bit about music.

The mysterious Rose, however, was about to face even more trouble when Jason, Eric and Fleece approached her in the Outer Space coffee bar next day. She was alone, sitting forlornly over a cup of coffee when they swaggered over to her.

'Your mates dropped you?' asked Jason.

'No.'

'Thought they might 'ave 'eard somethin'.'

'What about?' She looked up, alarmed.

'Your murky past.'

Rose immediately got up to go, but Eric's hand closed over her wrist. Abruptly she sat down.

'Don't go. We won't tell on you, will we, lads?'

'Course not,' said Jason.

'I mean, we wouldn't want them to jump to any wrong conclusions about that fiver you nicked.'

'I didn't take it.'

'I believe you, love,' said Eric smoothly. 'But the question is, will they? I mean, what will they think when they find out you've been done for that sort of thing a couple of times already? Don't worry, darling, we won't say anything about you.'

'Or your dad,' added Jason.

'You leave my dad out of it,' said Rose desperately.

Eric laughed. 'You can trust us, Rosie, can't she, lads?'

'You bet,' chorused the other two.

'What do you want?' asked Rose in a dead voice.

'Just a little favour,' said Eric softly.

'What kind of favour?'

'Information.'

'What sort?'

'Advance information.'

'No.' Again she tried to get up and again she found Eric's restraining hand on her arm.

'Course you're interested, Rosie,' said Eric in the same soft voice. 'Let's face it, it's in your own interests to be interested, isn't it? That is, of course, if you still want us to keep our mouths shut about the fact that you're on probation for thievin' and your old man's inside doin' six months.'

Preparations for the contest were busily going ahead

when Charlotte saw Rose coming into the clubroom. Charlotte was delighted to see her.

'Rosie, I thought you'd deserted us again.'

'You don't get rid of me that easily.'

'Have a cup of tea.'

'Thanks.'

When Charlotte returned with her cup, Rose said, 'All set for tonight, then?'

'I dunno about that, but we're goin' to get a good crowd in. All the kids at school have been talkin' about it.'

'So what are you doin' about drinks then?'

'Drinks?' Charlotte looked puzzled.

'Well, I mean, if there's all that lot comin', will you have enough?'

'No sweat. We've done a deal to get it on sale or return for the club.'

'Great.'

'Come along this afternoon if you like and give us a hand movin' the stuff.'

'I'll do just that,' said Rose, thoughtfully sipping her tea.

Knocker, urgently summoned from his home by Mac, glowered as he passed the players boarding the coach for the away match, Bobby Brent among them.

Once inside Mac's office, Knocker was at his most un-cooperative.

'You wanted me?'

''Bout half an hour ago, actually,' said Mac sourly.

'There didn't seem much point seeing I'm not playin'.'

'You are.'

'What?'

'You're playing in the A team today.'

Knocker stared at him in open disbelief. 'Now you've got to be jokin'.'

'No joke. The reserves don't have a game today, so it's going to *have* to be the A team.'

'You expect me to turn out with a bunch of kids?' exploded Knocker.

'Why not – I seem to remember Trevor Francis having to do that once.'

'Only I'm not Trevor Francis.'

'Is that supposed to cheer me up?'

'Very funny.'

'You'll find Syd Gregg waiting for you down in the dressing rooms. He's lookin' after the A team today.'

'Forget it.'

'Are you telling me that you're refusing to play in the A team?'

'I'll tell you what I'll do, boss. I will if he will.'

'Who?' grated Mac impatiently.

'Bobby Brent, of course, or is there one set of rules for him and one for the rest of us?'

'Look,' said Mac slowly, 'I'm not here to argue with you, son. You're in the A team and that's that. All right?'

'No, mate, it's not. In fact, it's anything but.' And he stormed out of the room, leaving a worried but resolute Mac staring down at his desk.

After watching the gang as they helped the steward to get crates of soft drinks and crisps out of the store, Eric and Fleece waited for their moment. It came when all was quiet and Jason lobbed a half-brick through the side window of the building. The steward heard the sound of breaking glass, left the store and hurried towards the noise. As he did so, Eric gave a quick signal to Jason who, running to a position behind the terraces, began to scream.

Directly he heard the infernal din that Jason was making, Fleece slipped into the still open door of the store, while the steward searched fruitlessly for the source of the appalling screams – that had now stopped.

Taking cover behind some crates, Fleece hid until the baffled steward returned. Shrugging, he closed the door, locked it and stared round him, still puzzled by the broken window and the commotion. Eric and Jason shook hands triumphantly, while inside, Fleece settled down to his long wait.

Dunmore lost the match badly without Knocker, and Mac, in face of Gregg's pseudo-sympathy, decided to be resolute by putting Knocker on the transfer list at once.

The kids were horrified at their team's 4–0 defeat, but went ahead with the disco with mounting excitement. Meanwhile, Gregg, angry at Mac's decision, cornered Rasputin, who had come down to watch the disco preparations, and led him outside to talk.

'You in favour of putting Knocker on the list after today's wipe-out?'

'It's up to Mac, isn't it?' asked Rasputin. 'No point in havin' a manager and barkin' yourself.'

'But it's Knocker's benefit season, for God's sake,' protested Gregg.

'He should have thought of that before throwin' punches at the club skipper.'

'That's the way you heard it, was it?' He gave Rasputin a knowing, wry grin.

'You tellin' me it wasn't?'

'Knocker says Bobby started it.'

'He would say that, wouldn't he?'

'Knocker's no liar. I've known him for years.'

'Why don't you tell Mac?'

'Because it's you that's goin' to be in trouble, Mr Chairman.'

'With who?'

'The Players' Union, of course.'

'Just because we've slapped a player on the transfer list?' Rasputin's voice was scornful.

'No. Because you've done it at the start of his benefit season. You can't do things like that without a damn good reason.'

'We've got one.'

'No, Mr Chairman. Two players get into a barney. One goes on the list, the other one gets away with it. It's not fair and Knocker's gonna say so.'

Rasputin looked at him sardonically. 'But you've got an axe to grind.'

Gregg shrugged. 'All I'm doing is trying to help you avoid trouble.'

Hiding in the shadows, Rose watched Eric and Jason move furtively towards the storeroom. Eric went up to the door and hissed, 'Fleecy?'

A muffled voice replied, 'Yeah?'

'Knock the alarm off, will you?'

'Sure.'

'Now,' said Eric turning to Jason, 'you got 'em?'

Silently, Jason produced the wire-cutters, and began to attack the padlock. After a while, he got through it and Eric opened the door. They went inside.

A few minutes later, Rose saw them emerge, cautiously wheeling trolleys. Then Eric went back, switched the alarm on and came out again. Then all three began heading towards a door marked EXECUTIVE BOX. They paused, Eric produced a key and then they stole inside.

Once she was sure they were all inside, Rose crept forward and hid behind the door just in time to hear Jason say:

'Where did you get the key?'

'Nicked it,' replied Eric, 'when they were cleanin' the place out the other day.'

'Why don't we just stick it in our van?' whispered Fleece.

'No,' said Eric, 'this is where we'll stash it. No one will think of looking for it here.'

But Jason had his finger to his lips and with one sudden, darting movement, he tugged open the door and Rose practically fell over the threshold. Before she had time to speak, Eric grabbed her, thrusting his face into hers.

'What's the idea?'

'I just wondered what was goin' on, that's all,' Rose gasped.

'Now you know.'

'Yeah.'

'And if you tell anyone –'

'But –'

'You'll be nicked along with us.'

'I haven't done nothin',' said Rose with a sob in her voice.

'We know that and you know that. But the police won't. Get me?'

Rose nodded fearfully and then Eric flung her away from him.

'Get lost,' he said.

'You look like you've seen a ghost,' said Charlotte.

Rose came into the clubroom to the barrage of sound from a group who were playing with more enthusiasm than accuracy.

'It's the heat,' she replied. 'Hot in here, isn't it?'

Just then, Eric, Jason and Fleece arrived and were met by a hostile Wurzel.

'Where the 'ell 'ave you lot been?'

'Out for a smoke,' said Eric.

'Well – you're on next – all right?'

'Our pleasure,' replied Eric, grinning at the other two. Then something caught his eye across the room. It was Rose's frightened face.

Eric, Jason and Fleece were just coming to the end of their number as Rasputin and Bobby Brent made notes at a table in the clubroom. Wurzel, Boxer, Charlotte and the rest of the mob sat watching stonily, but they were the only cloud of gloom; the rest of the kids in the audience were having a ball. When the number ended there was thunderous applause and Boxer, casting a jaundiced eye at Rasputin and Bobby, was annoyed to see them looking impressed. They turned to each other and began to talk animatedly. By this time, Wurzel had made his way on to the stage and taken the microphone.

'Right, everybody,' he began in a loud, commanding voice. 'That concludes tonight's heat. But don't forget – next Saturday night there's another heat and the winners of each heat go forward to our grand final in a month's time at Rasputin's Cave. And now, while our distinguished judges make up their minds, what about a bit of dancin'?'

Pacman, who was in charge of the turntable, put on a noisy dance record and the kids started to dance.

Meanwhile, Wurzel, Boxer and the rest of the gang made their way over to Rasputin and Bobby's table.

'Well. Only one contestant in it, I'd say. Right, Bobby?'

'Definitely.'

'You sure?' asked Boxer pointedly, but Bobby was very sure.

'They were great,' he said, looking across at Jason, Eric and Fleece who were surrounded by admiring fans. 'Look at the way the kids loved it.'

'Do I get the feelin' that you lot and that lot over there aren't what you might call blood brothers?' asked Rasputin mildly.

'Whatever gave you that idea?' replied Hulk innocently.

Rasputin gave him a suspicious glance. 'Good. Because I'd hate to think that you imagined me and Bobby here would let that influence our decision.'

'The thought never even crossed our minds, honest,' said Boxer guiltily.

'Good.' Rasputin gave him a mocking grin. 'In that case you'll not need me to tell you which one's goin' through to the grand final then.' He looked at Boxer who smiled weakly. 'I think it's pretty clear, don't you?'

Over in the corner, Jason was picking up his guitar case when Eric said abruptly, 'Knock it off, stupid!'

'Eh?'

'Leave the cases,' Eric rapped at him impatiently.

'Why – ?' Jason looked bewildered.

'Just leave 'em – all right?' grated Eric. Then he grinned and winked at him while Jason put his case down, wondering what Eric was up to.

Cassidy stood in front of the store, staring down at the damaged padlock. Then, with a swift movement, he took it off, pulled open the door and went hurriedly inside.

Once Cassidy had switched off the alarm, he saw a couple of empty beer bottles and half a dozen cigarette stubs lying on top of a beer crate next to a carton of cigarettes which had been torn open. Other cartons were strewn about the place.

'Blimey,' he said aloud, pausing indecisively and staring down at the mess. Then he turned back to the door and began to run. But as he emerged breathlessly from the store, he bumped straight into Jud and immediately grabbed him.

'Got you!'

'Eh?' Jud looked flabbergasted as Cassidy's hands plucked at his shirt collar.

'Coming back for the rest of it, eh?'

'I was just nipping round to the Junior Supporters' Club, that's all.'

'On a Monday morning?'

'I'm not at school today . . .' replied Jud defensively.

'Try telling that to the police,' said Cassidy in tones of ice.

'I don't know what you mean —' Jud started to back off but Cassidy took him by the arm and propelled him towards the offices.

Jud was playing pool in the clubhouse when the door opened and Cassidy came in with P.C. Greenway. Reluctantly, Cassidy had agreed to Mac's view that Jud should remain unrestrained on the premises until the police arrived. Mac trusted kids too much, reckoned Cassidy. But this should teach him a lesson.

'This is the lad I was telling you about, Constable. The one I found lurking about in our store.' Cassidy was all righteous indignation.

'That's a flamin' lie!' said Jud hotly.

'All right, son, that's enough of that,' said P.C. Greenway with quiet authority. 'Right, thanks, Mr Cassidy. If you'll just leave it to me now.'

Looking disappointed, Cassidy left the room and the Constable turned to Jud gravely.

'O.K., son, let's talk,' he said.

But despite close questioning Jud for half an hour, P.C. Greenway could find no evidence to link him with the theft. Much to Cassidy's irritation, he let him go, leaving Mac, Rasputin and Cassidy to consider the knotty problem of how the store was burgled without the alarm going off. After a while they realized that someone must have hidden inside to turn the alarm off. But what they couldn't make out was how the burglar had got hold of the key to the alarm which was always on Cassidy's person. But then Cassidy had haltingly admitted that because he couldn't be available every time the store was opened, he left the key in the alarm – a fact that went down like a ton of bricks with Rasputin, who was thinking of what his insurance company was going to say.

Meanwhile, the crooks were having a discreet conference in the Outer Space coffee bar.

'So when are we goin' to get the stuff out then?' asked Fleece.

'I told you – when it's safe,' said Eric patiently.

'And when's that goin' to be?'

'Well, certainly not today – with the fuzz crawlin' all over the woodwork down there.'

'So when, then, Eric?' put in Jason hopefully.

'Tomorrow – when you've finished at school,' said Eric. 'Soon as the Junior Supporters' Club opens for business.'

'The Junior Supporters' Club? What the 'ell 'ave they got to do with it?'

Eric smiled. 'They're goin' to provide us with the perfect excuse for bein' down there, aren't they?'

'How?' Jason was once again mystified by his brother's plans.

'Well – why else did you think I left our guitar cases down there the other night? So that when things had died down a bit we could go along there and collect 'em. All perfectly legit.' He gave Jason and Fleece a smug look.

'Oh, I see,' replied Jason.

'I wish I did,' said Fleece.

Eric gave him a pained look. 'Listen – we've got all these thousands of ciggies stashed away down there, where nobody would think of searchin', right?'

'Right.' Fleece nodded.

'And what we've also got down there at the moment are two big fat empty guitar cases. Now then. What's one of the very clever ways in which you could use that situation to get your ill-gotten gains out of there?'

'Stick the ciggies in the guitar cases!' said Fleece with sudden comprehension.

'Brilliant.' Eric turned to Fleece questioningly. 'In fact I wonder sometimes, Fleecy, how you've gone all these years without bein' spotted for that programme, you know.'

'What programme?' asked Fleece innocently.

'Mastermind,' replied Eric.

Rasputin's worries about the robbery and his insurance company were suddenly interrupted by a different problem of rather greater magnitude. The entire Dunmore team had just walked out. With considerable concern, Rasputin asked Mac to come to his office. When he arrived, he gloomily explained the situation and said, 'I suppose it does have to be admitted that they have a point.'

'What point would that be?' asked Mac gently.

'Well, the obvious one. I mean, two players get involved in a fight and one of 'em gets ticked off. The other one gets slapped on the transfer list.'

Mac gave him a withering look. 'Look, you know as well as I do that wasn't the only reason Clarkey was put on the list. He's an assassin on the field and a trouble-maker off it. If it hadn't been that it would have been something else.'

'So what a pity you didn't wait for something else.'

'What do you mean by that?'

'What the 'ell does it look like?'

'Look, to hell with what it looks like! All that concerns me is what it is!'

'And what concerns me, mate, is that we do just happen to have a Milk Cup First Round Cup-Tie next weekend and my entire first team squad have just walked out on me.'

Mac could see that Rasputin was beginning to lose his temper. 'If the first team won't turn out, we'll field the second team,' he said firmly.

Rasputin was not to be appeased. 'Terrific. Here we are, up to our armpits in debt, and you want us to commit hara-kiri in the First Round of what could be our only decent moneyspinner of the season.'

'What the hell else can we do?'

Rasputin looked at him speculatively. 'There is one thing we could do, I suppose. I mean, to cut the ground from under those screams of "victimization".'

'What could I do?'

'List Bobby Brent as well.'

There was a long silence. Then Mac said, 'You *have* to be joking.'

'No, I'm not joking.'

'On what grounds would I list Bobby Brent?'

'He was fightin' too. It takes two to tango, mate . . .'

'He was provoked!' said Mac grimly.

'Well, have you got a better suggestion?' asked Rasputin challengingly.

'Just one.' He got up.

'Well?'

'Why don't I go instead?'

'Don't be stupid . . .'

'Nobody's being stupid. Look, the way I see it, it's either Knocker or me. Now quite obviously you aren't keen to let him go. Not if it means trouble with the rest of his mates in the first team. So let me solve your problem for you. I'll go. You can have my resignation first thing tomorrow morning.'

Rasputin then exploded into a rush of angry words. 'You're flamin' well doin' it again! The minute anybody round here so much as dares to suggest you could just be wrong about something – you immediately start wavin' your resignation under my nose! And you know, you want to watch it, mate – 'cos one of these days I might just accept it.'

'So do us both a favour, Mr Chairman. Do it now!' Mac snapped.

'Don't push me too far, Mac. I'm warnin' you.'

'Like I said. First thing tomorrow morning.' With that Mac walked quickly out of the office, leaving Rasputin to kick the waste-paper basket across the room.

Mac was sitting reading in his living room when the doorbell rang. When he answered it, he found Syd Gregg standing on his doorstep, looking pleased with himself.

'Hallo, Mac.'

'Can I help you?'

'I've only called in for a minute. All I wanted to say was – no hard feelings, I hope.'

'Hard feelings?' Mac looked mystified.

'About me taking over.'

'You?'

'You did know, didn't you? That Rasputin had asked me to take over?' He was practically smacking his lips with the pleasure of telling him.

'As a matter of fact, I didn't.'

'Oh dear . . .' He looked both surprised and embarrassed but his expression was strictly phoney.

'But don't let it worry you,' said Mac. 'I mean, after all – what's it to me who takes over? I'm the one who resigned, remember?' He looked at Gregg coldly.

'Yeah, I know, but – well, I'd rather it hadn't been me though.'

'Like I said – don't worry about it. All the best to you in your new job.'

'Thanks, Mac. Yeah, well, like I said – that's all I came for really.'

'And it's appreciated. Believe me.'

'Oh, good. So, I'll be seeing you then. Soon, eh?'

'I'll look forward to it,' said Mac, gently closing the door in Syd Gregg's slightly bemused face.

But Gregg's satisfaction was short-lived, for directly he returned to the ground he was called to Rasputin's new office, only to see Wurzel hurriedly leaving. He scuttled past Gregg with an anxious look and, as he knocked on Rasputin's door, Gregg felt a sudden unease.

'You wanted a word, Mr Jones?'

'Yeah, I did, Syd. Have a pew.' He looked elaborately casual. 'I've been having a word with young Wurzel.'

'Oh, yeah?'

'Apparently, him and his mates saw you having a meeting.'

'Meeting?' asked Gregg with a sinking heart.

'The one you called yesterday for the senior playin' staff – after which the entire bunch of 'em walked out.'

'The meeting I called, Mr Jones?' repeated Gregg.

'Are you tellin' me that you didn't? Are you sayin' all them kids are wrong?'

Gregg looked at him, warily determined to talk himself out of the situation. 'There was trouble brewing. Somebody had to do something.'

'I agree with you,' said Rasputin calmly. 'But you should have gone to Mac Murphy and warned him about it or come to me.' Then his voice hardened. 'But you decided not to bother doin' either of those things, didn't you, Sydney? You called a meetin' of the players and, from the sound of it, made things a damn sight worse.'

'Knocker Clarke felt that he had a legitimate grievance and I happened to agree with him,' said Gregg defensively.

'All right. So that was your opinion and you had a right to it. What you don't have any right to do as a member of the management team is to go callin' meetings behind the manager's back and stirring it for him.'

'You 'ave no proof I did anything of the kind. You've only listened to a bunch of kids.'

'And in this case – I believe 'em.'

Gregg began to bluster. 'Knocker Clarke's going to lose thousands of pounds if he gets transferred away from his club during his benefit season.'

But Rasputin was all too prepared to nip that little ploy in the bud. 'Knocker Clarke won't lose a penny out of the move and you can have my personal guarantee on that. In fact, as far as I'm concerned it'll be money well spent – just to get rid of him, seein' that his kind of football just doesn't happen to be welcome round here any more. So why don't you call another of those cosy little meetings of yours and tell him that? Make it clear to him and to the rest of the first team that nobody's bein' victimized and nobody's going to lose any money – and if that still isn't good enough for 'em, tell 'em from me they can all go on the list!'

'And what about me? Where does that leave me then?' He looked flabbergasted.

'You're welcome to stay, Sydney – as deputy manager. I mean, we wouldn't want you runnin' round screamin' "victimization", would we? Unless, of course, you were thinkin' of resignin' on principle.'

Gregg gave him a very bitter grin. 'You'll be hearing from my solicitors – you realize that, don't you?'

'Yes,' said Rasputin. 'I realized that.'

Gregg stormed out while Rasputin sat at his desk for a moment. Then he picked up the phone and began to dial Mac's number.

The gang were sitting around in the clubhouse, disconsolately listening to records, when Eric, Jason and Fleece strolled arrogantly in.

'Bit early, aren't you?' said Boxer. 'The finals aren't for another month yet.'

'We came to pick up our guitar cases,' said Eric brusquely.

Boxer looked around him and saw the cases in a corner.

'All right?' asked Eric.

Boxer shrugged, stepping out of their way. 'I s'pose so,' he said grudgingly as they picked up the cases and carried them outside.

'Wonder what they're up to?' asked Boxer, and the kids looked suspiciously at each other.

Knocker was angrily packing his kit into a holdall in the Dunmore dressing room. With him was Gregg, hoping to work him into a better mood. But it was an uphill struggle.

'Knocker,' said Gregg tentatively.

'Yeah?' But he hardly looked up at him.

'I'm sorry I couldn't do more for you.'

'That makes two of us, doesn't it?'

'At least you won't lose anything by it – and anyway, a change of club might do you good.'

But Knocker was not going to have any soft soap and he turned on him savagely. 'Do you really think that's what matters, eh? Do you?'

'What do you mean?'

'He fixed me. The Scottish git. But don't worry, mate. He has it comin', one way or the other. You'll see ...' Unable to stand Gregg's company any longer, Knocker pushed past him and slammed out of the dressing room.

But when Knocker came hurtling out of the offices and into the car park, his temper rose when he discovered that he was blocked in by Eric's gaudily painted van. Knocker glared at the vehicle, noticing the back doors were open, as was the nearby gate in the wall of the football ground. Angrily, Knocker stalked through the gate to look for the driver. He was going to give him hell.

'You still got the key?' said Jason uneasily as they stood outside the directors' box with their guitar cases.

'What do you think?' asked Eric contemptuously, producing the key and beginning to unlock the door. Suddenly they froze as a voice bellowed:

'Oi, you lot! Come 'ere a minute!'

'Let's go!' said Eric with sudden decision and they legged it in a hurry in the opposite direction.

Knocker stood there staring after them in surprise. Then he made his way towards the open door and slowly went inside.

When his eyes became used to the dim light he saw the stolen cigarette cartons in the trolleys and suddenly realized what he had found.

'Well,' he said softly. 'This must be my lucky day.'

Knocker began to gather the cartons together on one trolley. When he had finished, he peered cautiously around, saw that the coast was clear and slowly began to wheel the trolley out, looking furtively to right and left as he went.

As he loaded the cartons into his car, Knocker suddenly noticed a familiar vehicle parked nearby – it was Mac's. After a few seconds' contemplation, Knocker suddenly had another brilliant idea. Cautiously, he tried Mac's boot, found it open – and quickly tossed in three cartons of cigarettes. Then he slammed it shut and returned to his own car, grinning.

As he drove away, Knocker muttered to himself, 'That'll fix him.'

Ten minutes later, Knocker stopped his car outside a telephone box. He hurried in and began to dial. When a voice answered, he said briskly, 'Hallo, is that the police? I've got some information for you – about some stolen goods.'

'Blimey,' said Boxer as he and Wurzel walked down the street towards the Dunmore ground. 'Look at that.'

Mac was walking towards his parked car, accompanied by Rasputin – and P.C. Greenway. Even from this distance, both Boxer and Wurzel could detect the tension. Walking slowly on, they hung around, just within ear-shot.

'The boot, you say?' said Mac as they arrived at the car.

'If you don't mind, sir,' said P.C. Greenway.

'Now look, this is flamin' ridiculous . . .' began Rasputin, but P.C. Greenway cut across him.

'Quite possibly, sir. At the same time, we have had a complaint, so we do have to check it out. So if you will just open the boot, sir . . .'

Mac opened the boot and looked. There in the back were three packs of cigarettes. Boxer and Wurzel craned their necks but they still could not see inside the boot. But they could see Mac's face change expression dramatically.

'Well, well,' he said, 'will you look what I've found?'

'Yours, are they, sir?'

'I've never seen them before in my life!'

'Well, of course he hasn't!' yelled Rasputin. 'You can't seriously be suggesting that Mac took the flamin' cigarettes!'

'At this stage, sir, I'm not suggesting anything,' replied P.C. Greenway gloomily. 'Merely making inquiries. So, tell you what – why don't we go back to the office, sir? We can discuss it there.'

Rasputin was about to argue further, but then he saw Boxer and Wurzel standing nearby, obviously listening.

'Yeah,' he said quietly, 'why don't we do that? Then we can leave you to get on with findin' out who really nicked my cigarettes . . .'

But as Mac was about to close the boot, P.C. Greenway took the cigarettes out of the boot and said, 'You will, of course, get a receipt for these.'

'Thank you,' said Mac grimly.

'Oh – by the way, could I just warn you, sir, that anything you do say will be taken down in writing and may be used in evidence against you?'

Mac stared at him in disbelief. 'This is the first time I've laid eyes on those damned things!'

'I'll make a note of that, sir.' He indicated the way back to the office. 'Shall we go and have our little chat, sir?'

Reluctantly, Mac and Rasputin made their way back towards the office door, accompanied by P.C. Greenway, while Boxer and Wurzel looked at one another in horror.

A few minutes later, Boxer and Wurzel found the trolley standing outside the ground. Absent-mindedly, they wheeled it in – only to be confronted by an enraged Cassidy who pointed out to them that the trolley belonged to the liquor store – and that it had been stolen along with the goods. He then proceeded to hint darkly that they just might have had something to do with the burglary – using the noisy disco as a cover. The shock of this accusation, on top of what they had heard about Mac, made Boxer and Wurzel call an immediate club conference.

'Do you reckon the police will come round then?' asked Hulk curiously, when they had explained both sagas and a vote of confidence in Mac's innocence had been taken.

'About what?' snapped Boxer. 'All we did was find the thing, wasn't it?'

'Old Cassidy does have a point, though, doesn't he?' said Pacman.

'What point?' asked Jud aggressively.

'Well, I mean, if that trolley was the one the burglars nicked – how come it's turned up outside the gates again, all of a sudden?'

''Cos obviously that's where the thieves left it, wasn't it?

When they'd finished with it the other night,' said Mugsy, with a professional air.

'Come on – if they had, we'd have noticed it before now, wouldn't we?' said Wurzel reasonably.

'Course we would,' put in Charlotte. 'And anyway, if we 'adn't, Cassidy and the police would have. I mean, they've been lookin' for it too, haven't they?'

'This afternoon is the first time the trolley's surfaced again – what does that tell you?' asked Boxer.

'What?' Mugsy looked completely baffled.

'It tells you that somebody was using it to move stuff again, that's what!' said Boxer patiently.

'You mean – you think somebody's been havin' another go at the store then?' asked Hulk.

'No, that's not what I mean at all,' said Boxer. 'Look, just supposin' when they'd actually got their hands on the cigarettes, it wasn't really safe to move it there and then?'

'Right,' replied Pacman.

'So what would you have done if you'd been them?'

'Stashed it away on the ground somewhere,' said Jud.

Boxer nodded eagerly. 'Where you could come and pick it up again later – once all the fuss had died down a bit.'

'"Later" in this case being this afternoon, maybe,' said Charlotte. 'If all of a sudden the trolley's turned up again.'

'Right! So whoever nicked the stuff was almost certainly back on the ground this afternoon doin' just that . . .'

There was a pregnant silence, then everybody started talking at once.

'So, all right, hang on a minute – LISTEN, will yer!' yelled Jud and they quietened down. 'When you lot were comin' on here this afternoon, did anybody see anybody, anybody at all, hangin' about the place?'

The kids all looked at one another and shrugged.

'If that is what they were doin', of course. Hangin' about . . .' said Wurzel.

'What do you mean?' asked Charlotte.

'Well, what I mean is – you wouldn't need to be hangin' about, would you? Not if you had a perfectly good reason for being on the ground in the first place.'

'And what sort of reason would that be?' Boxer looked puzzled.

'Well,' continued Wurzel, 'suppose you'd been here on Saturday night at the disco – which by an amazin' coincidence was just goin' on at about the same time the store was bein' robbed, as Mr Cassidy was so kind to point out. And when you left that night, you left something behind that would just need to be picked up later in the week.'

'Like what, for instance?' asked Jud.

'Like a couple of empty guitar cases, for instance?'

There was a total silence. Then Charlotte said, 'But, of course! Jason and that brother of his! They were here this afternoon . . . !'

'Yeah,' said Jud angrily, 'and what better way of carryin' stolen cigarettes around than in a guitar case?'

'Yeah, but hang on a minute, hang on!' said Boxer. 'There's just one thing wrong with that though, isn't there? Why would they need a trolley, if they were moving the stolen ciggies in their guitar cases?'

Everyone groaned as they saw his logic.

'I don't know why,' said Wurzel unabashed. 'But I'll tell you what else I don't know – I don't know why they had to leave the guitar cases in the first place, do you?'

'So why don't we find Jason an' the Argonauts an' ask 'em why, right?' asked Jud aggressively and there were cheers of support.

'I'll buy that,' said Boxer. 'So, where do we find them? Does anybody know?'

'Well, Rose would, I suppose . . .' put in Charlotte.

'Ask Rose,' said Wurzel.

It didn't take the gang long to get the truth out of Rose. But when she had admitted to Jason and the Argonauts' involvement, Charlotte pressed her still further. Why did she go on seeing them? Why did she protect them? Then the tragic answer emerged. Rose's dad was in prison and Jason had told her he would spread the bad news around unless she kept her mouth shut.

Furious, the gang set out to track down the Argonauts, leaving Charlotte to reassure Rose that it didn't make a bit of difference to her – or any of the gang – that her dad was inside.

Finally they ran them to earth in an amusement arcade.

Mugsy said, 'Over there, in the corner.'

Eric, Jason and Fleece were laughing noisily about something and hovering over a machine. But their laughter soon died away when they suddenly found the gang standing there looking at them with hostility.

'Hallo again,' said Boxer menacingly.

'What do *you* want?' asked Jason warily.

'Just a word, about those ciggies that went missin'.'

'Ciggies? There must be some mistake, mate,' said Eric quickly. 'I don't smoke myself. What about you, Jace, do you smoke?'

'What, me? After what our old lady said? You're jokin', big brother.'

Eric smiled wistfully. 'Our old lady was always dead nuts

against ciggies. Do whatever else you want to, she used to say – but keep away from ciggies.'

Boxer smiled. 'So you lot know nothing about them then. Right?'

'That's right,' replied Eric.

'Then you've nothin' to worry about, 'ave you? We'll just pass on what we know to the police and let them sort it out with you.'

There was a long silence while Eric looked grimly at Jason and Fleece. Boxer strolled off. Then, making a decision, Eric went after him. 'What are you on about?' he said.

'You 'eard 'im – ciggies,' put in Jud. 'Them things your old lady warned you about.'

'I'm tellin' you, we know nothin' about any ciggies.'

'Then like I've just told you – you're in the clear, aren't you?' insisted Boxer.

'So what's all this about the police then?' Fleece still looked alarmed.

Wurzel began to explain. 'What he means is – the police are naturally interested, aren't they? In anything or anybody who might just be able to 'elp them with their inquiries. Like anybody who might have been at the Junior Supporters' Club the night of the break-in.'

Charlotte continued, 'And was around again today, when whoever it was hid the stuff on the ground came round to collect it.'

'Anybody with a couple of empty guitar cases, say,' wound up Boxer. 'Well – empty, that is, when they arrived. We couldn't of course swear what they 'ad in them when they left ...'

'Now just a minute,' began Eric. 'Let's talk, all right? Look, what's it to you who nicked the fags, anyway? I mean, what are you – a copper's grass or something?'

'No, mate,' said Boxer. 'Just a friend of Mac Murphy's, that's all. We don't want to see him slagged for something he didn't do.'

'Mac Murphy? What the hell's he got to do with it?'

'Some of the cigarettes turned up in his car.'

'What?' He looked genuinely surprised.

'Yeah. And then somebody told the coppers if they looked they'd find 'em there.'

'We didn't do it! Why the 'ell should we?'

'You tell me.'

'I'm tellin' you, it wasn't us!' Eric was very insistent.

'If it wasn't you, who was it then? Or shall we leave it to the police to ask you about it?'

Eric stared at him, knowing he was trapped – and Boxer grinned.

'Look, if I tell you, will you promise to keep our names out of it? 'Cos I'm tellin' you now, we came out of this with nothin'.'

'Dunno about that,' said Boxer warily.

'Take it or leave it, if you want to know who did it, that's the best offer you're gonna get.'

Boxer hesitated and then said, 'Start talkin'.'

Lowering his voice, Eric began to tell him about Knocker.

Boxer had to give his word not to split on the Argonauts – and so did the rest of the gang, albeit unwillingly. So the problem was – now they knew about Knocker's involvement, what were they going to do about it? Then Wurzel's fertile imagination came into play and half an hour later Boxer was sweating it out in a telephone box – hoping Wurzel's idea would work.

'Is that Knocker Clarke?' said Boxer nervously.

'Yeah?'

'It's about them cigarettes, Knocker. The ones you nicked from us down at the ground the other day ...'

'Who is this?'

'I've told you – one of the kids you chased off yesterday.'

'Look, sonny. I don't know what your game is, but I haven't a blind idea what you're talking about,' said Knocker sounding furious.

But Boxer kept calm. 'I'm on about cigarettes, Mr Clarke. Cigarettes that you nicked from us. Oh, that is, apart from the couple of packs you left in Mac Murphy's car. To make it look like he'd done it.'

'Just what do you want from me?' He was guarded now.

'Let's talk about it, eh? I mean, we're not greedy. Maybe we can come to some arrangement. Help you get rid of 'em, maybe? Look, I'll tell you what. We'll meet you somewhere. Say the place where you found we'd stashed the cigarettes, all right?'

'When?' asked Knocker suspiciously.

'Tonight. Say about – six o'clock? What do you say?'

'I'll see you there,' said Knocker and put the phone down abruptly, leaving Boxer leaning on the glass door of the telephone kiosk in exhaustion. So far so good, he thought. But in fact the worst was to come.

At the appointed time Boxer was sitting on the edge of a table inside the directors' box. After what seemed like an eternity the door opened, making him jump and almost fall off the table in nervous agitation. Then he saw it was Charlotte.

'His car's just arrived outside the offices.'

'Right.'

'You O.K.?'

'Fine.'

'Good luck then.'

'Thanks, Charlie.' He winked at her and she closed the door again. Then, after more agonizing minutes, Knocker arrived. But when he saw Boxer sitting there he looked surprised.

'You?'

'S'right.'

Knocker stared at him, not knowing what to do. 'I don't remember seein' you here,' he said suspiciously.

'There's a reason for that, Knocker. I wasn't here.' He gave a nervous grin. 'See – I'm what you might call the mastermind behind the jobs we do, know what I mean?'

Knocker stared at him calculatingly, still unsure. 'What do you want?' he said softly and Boxer realized again just how dangerous the situation was becoming.

'Just our fair share. After all – we nicked the fags first, so we must be due something. Right?'

'And if I don't agree? Then what?'

Boxer swallowed. 'You know what ...' But his threat sounded hollow.

'You tip off the police. Right?'

'Right.'

'Only if you did that, you'd incriminate yourselves.'

'We'd say we'd seen you nicking the stuff. Our word against yours.'

Knocker moved in suddenly and grabbed Boxer by the front of his shirt, nearly lifting him off the ground. 'Do you know what I think, son? I think you're bluffing ...'

'No ...'

'Bluffing! Trying to make a monkey out of me!' He threw Boxer against the wall. 'I don't like people who try to make a monkey out of me. In fact, it makes me mad. Flaming mad!'

Boxer lay on the floor looking up at Knocker. He was very afraid for there was a murderous look in the man's eyes. Slowly he began to edge away from him, but Knocker, smiling grimly, walked threateningly towards him. Just as he was about to grab him the door burst open and Mac, the kids and Rasputin stood there.

Knocker swung round and for a moment it looked as if he was going to hit Mac.

Mac grinned savagely. 'Go on. Just give me an excuse – please . . .'

Knocker stood still, his arms by his sides, suddenly looking defeated.

'Now,' said Rasputin, 'how about a little visit to the nick?'

Rose stood timidly at the door of the hall, just underneath a banner which garishly proclaimed: SEARCH FOR A STAR. She stared around, watching the swarming kids setting up posters and tables. Then she saw Boxer deep in conversation with Jud, but they were both far too busy to take any notice of her. Rose hesitated again and then, with sudden decision, walked in.

On stage there was a group rehearsing a number, while Pacman and Hulk fiddled around with a microphone, making a terrible din. Then Charlotte spotted her.

'Rose! Hi!' said Charlotte in delight, hurrying over to her.

'Hi!' Rose replied nervously.

'Come on and meet some of the others.' Charlotte led her towards the other girls, who crowded around Rose in a friendly fashion. Suddenly Rose's spirits lifted. She was wanted.

*

Mac sat down next to Rasputin on the judges' table.

'Blimey! If I 'adn't seen it with my very own eyes, I wouldn't 'ave believed it. You've turned up!' He looked amazed.

'Yeah – I must be out of my mind . . .'

'Come on – least you can do is a bit of judgin'. After what this mob did for you a couple of weeks ago.' Then he said, 'Elaine's not come with you then?'

'Babysitting.'

'You don't know how lucky you are. Havin' a girl like that to put you back on the straight and narrow – every time you do your Scottish nut.'

'Do you think so?'

'She did tell you, did she, that I rang her and suggested she had a word with you? When you was thinkin' of leavin' us a fortnight ago?'

'Oh aye. Matter of fact she rang me. The same night.'

'Well, thank heavens somebody can make you see a bit of sense occasionally.'

'Her advice was to tell you what to do with the job and catch the next plane out to Aussie . . .'

'What? You're lyin' . . .' Rasputin turned on him angrily.

Mac was grinning.

'You will 'ave your little joke, won't you?' Rasputin said, giving Mac a friendly punch.

'So thanks a bunch, pal.' Boxer was standing with Jud when Eric tapped him on the shoulder. Just behind stood Jason and Fleece, looking aggrieved.

'So what's your problem then?' Boxer was tense, ready for trouble.

'You promised to keep our names out of it.'

'I did.'

'So how come we're getting nicked then?' whined Jason.

Boxer shrugged. ''Cos Knocker Clarke wasn't goin' to go down on his own, was he?'

'Not to mention all the good work Fleece did on your behalf,' put in Jud.

'What are you on about?' asked Fleece aggressively.

'What I'm on about, mate, is the full collection of dabs which you did just happen to leave all over those bottles of beer you were swiggin', the night they left you in the liquor store.'

'Yeah,' said Boxer joyfully, 'which matched up beautifully, accordin' to Wurzel's dad, with some they already 'ad of yours on the computer . . .'

Eric and Jason turned to look at Fleece who tried to smile. But the smile vanished when Eric said, 'We got some talkin' to do.'

'Have we?' asked Fleece nervously.

'Oh yes,' replied Eric grimly, 'a lot of talkin'.'

An hour later, the group had really got going and so had the dancing. Rose stood alone, watching all the fun, until Wurzel tapped her on the shoulder. 'Free for this one, are you?'

'Yeah.' She looked surprised and then delighted.

Charlotte stood watching them, grinning, until Jud and Boxer arrived at exactly the same moment – and both asked her to dance. She looked at them, nonplussed for a moment. Then she said, 'I think this was where I came in, wasn't it?'

They all began to laugh.

On the platform, Rasputin said to Mac, 'Not a bad bunch of kids – I s'pose.'

'You watch out,' said Mac grimly. 'Wait till you see what they get up to next.'

'What *are* they getting up to next?' asked Rasputin nervously.

'I don't know,' said Mac, 'but it'll be something.'

MURPHY'S MOB
Michael Saunders

Dunmore United is anchored firmly in the Fourth Division, and the facilities are terrible. The old run-down ground is now the haunt of all the local tearaways – kids like Gerry, Boxer, Wurzel and the Prof.

But when Mac Murphy, ex-star, ex-First Division Manager, takes charge, things begin to change, not just on the pitch but off it too. One of his first ideas is to let the kids form their own Supporters' Club. Some people say it's the worst decision he ever made – but Murphy's Mob are determined to prove him right.

MURPHY & CO.
Anthony Masters

Money is still short at Dunmore United, so the Junior Supporters' Club – the Mob – decide to help out. But their efforts look puny beside the half a million which someone else comes up with. *Half a million*? The Mob smell a rat and decide to find out just what's going on.

*Both books are based on the television
series by Brian Finch*

BRIAN GLANVILLE'S BOOK OF FOOTBALLERS

Using his incomparable world-wide knowledge of the game, Brian Glanville has compiled an alphabetical guide to great footballers, past and present, European and South American. Many contemporary stars from around the world have been included: Kempes, Maradona, Platini, Rummenigge, Socrates, Zico – and many others. Every football-lover will find it invaluable.

FROM SCHOOLBOY TO SUPERSTAR
Patrick Barclay

What does it take to become a professional footballer? And just how do you set about joining a club? Through a series of interviews with stars like Steve Coppell, Dennis Tueart and Sammy Lee, Patrick Barclay shows what you need to make the grade . . . and, just as important, how to ensure that your life doesn't fall apart if you don't quite make it as a footballer.

JOHNNY JARVIS
Nigel Williams

Johnny Jarvis was the sort of kid who did everything right: stuck by his mum and dad, got an apprenticeship, worked hard. Other kids were out of work, but he'd be all right, wouldn't he? His best mate was Alan Lipton, layabout and cynic, but clever. This is the story of Johnny and his girl, told in the words of Alan Lipton. It's also the story of a bent copper and a deal that went sour. (A recent BBC TV series.)

THE DEVIL ON THE ROAD
Robert Westall

Pottering round the bit of Suffolk where Chance and his Triumph Tiger-Cub had landed him for the summer, John Webster found himself with a lot of unanswered questions. Why was the local squire so keen for him to stay on in the old barn? Why were the villagers behaving so deferentially? If he'd known the answers to those questions, that little village wouldn't have seen John for dust. As it was, he had to find out the hard way.